Weapons of Choice

ThrillHers Anthology

Deb Collins   Sonja Dewing   Pat McGregor

Michelle Tennant Nicholson   Amy Rivers   Kara Smith

Ursula Vogt

Plot Duckies

Foreword

Life is sometimes stranger than fiction! The theme for this anthology was decided after Deb Collins's husband found a gun under a pillow at a hotel (and it wasn't his)!

Just a few months after that, I found a gun lying around in my neighborhood. At first, I thought it wasn't real, but I picked it up, and the weight of it told me it was real. It was a 9mm pistol in a plastic holster.

Yikes! It's a good thing we're just writers and not nefarious never-do-wells who could have done a lot of damage with those weapons (they are now in the hands of their owner and the police). But they certainly got the ideas flowing.

Weapons became a topic of discussion for the Women's Thriller Writers Association, as well as the theme. And this theme certainly inspired some amazing stories!

Foreword

Each story focuses on a different weapon - from money to an icicle and in directions I hope that surprise you! Seven stories from seven amazing authors!

Happy thrill reading!

Sonja Dewing

Table of Contents

The FBI is sending a forensic expert to help. In the meantime, the town psychic swears that a ghostly presence is haunting us. She could be right. I've lived here forty years and have never seen anything like this. As the sheriff, I need to put a stop to it. - Mora Gentry.

***Misdirection* by Pat McGregor** - Ripped from the headlines, Pat McGregor's *"Misdirection"* leads Health Department investigator Magnolia Mbele on a merry chase through diners & drive-ins, searching for the poisoner who's picking victims at random and adulterating their food. When the poisoner strikes close to home, will Magnolia be able to catch her villain before death takes her mother?

***What Satisfies Hunger* by Amy Rivers -** Sharon wants nothing to do with her family, especially after her torturous life with her daddy. Unexpectedly, her daddy left her the house. Meanwhile, her half-sister is desperate to get her hands on it, over her dead body.

***Winterovers* by Kara Smith** - There is something not right at the South Pole, and Alice is determined to find out what. When a former classmate offers her a high-profile assignment at the remote South Pole Station, she jumps at the chance for a fresh start. But upon arrival, the tight-lipped staff's lack of cooperation and mysterious events signal that something sinister is happening beneath the ice.

***The Cairn's Curse* by Michelle Tennant Nicholson** - When Michelle, Shannon, and their friends visit Moab, Utah, for an adventurous getaway, a simple mistake shatters the peace of the desert. One friend innocently moves an ancient cairn, unknowingly unleashing the wrath of long-dormant spirits tied to sacred burial grounds. As eerie events unfold, the group must survive a flash flood in the dangerous Mary Jane Slot Canyon and confront a curse older than time. Haunted by their misstep, they seek a way to restore balance, knowing their survival depends on more than just skill—it requires reverence for the land's ancient guardians. Will they make it out alive, or will the desert claim them?

***Good for the Game* by Ursula Vogt** - An investors meeting to celebrate a record-breaking year is about to take place on board a luxury gambling yacht just off the Miami coast. But it's no ordinary company, and this is no ordinary meeting. Welcome aboard the Love Thy Neighbor, where the sun is hot, the drinks are cold, and the stakes are high. But who wins and who loses is no game of chance for any of them.

Plenty of Ammunition
Deb Collins

I should have just stayed out of it. Stayed out of the whole damn thing. But Tom was something special; something amazing; something so exhilarating I couldn't shake. I was obsessed with him, and I hated him.

To say that night was dark and rainy would be an understatement. What had looked to be a passing downpour had turned into a true Texas thunderstorm. The blue sky clouded over with a greyness that native Texans knew meant business. Within a matter of ten minutes, the sky blackened, and the wind picked up thirty miles per hour. The curtain of rain couldn't be detected until it was upon you — the kind of storm where you don't see even one raindrop until complete sheets of rain are pelleting your windshield. It was that all-encompassing. And then came the hail, plinking onto car hoods and windshields and roofs in ping-pong-sized balls, sounding as innocent as change being dropped into a child's piggy bank. Usually, these storms lasted just a matter of minutes, bringing thunder like a head-on freight train that rumbles to your very core and flash-flooding roads and land that are so used to a drought they've forgotten how to absorb water.

My wipers were useless as I followed Tom to the cabin near Lake Caddo. It was a cabin he'd rented at least once before. He'd brought me there once too, long ago. If he'd asked, I would have gone a second, third, and fourth time.

Tom's deep, velvet voice had a way of slipping me into a trance. I drowned in his green-hazel eyes. I knew we had something special. In and out of bed. But that weekend we'd shared at the cabin had been mostly in. He'd told his wife he was out of town on business. As a career FBI agent, Tom never had to give much explanation as to his whereabouts. Then after that perfect forty-eight hours, as he dropped me off, he'd turned to me and said simply, "I'm sorry, Abby. I can't do this to Char." Insinuating that I could.

So much did I love Charlotte that I'd tried hard to understand. To stay away from him. But I'd wanted to punish Tom for his choices – for not only turning away from me, but also for marrying the wrong sister in the first place. I wore low-cut, tight clothing whenever Charlotte invited me over. Even to babysit my baby nephew. Tom would notice and sometimes even reward me with a wink behind Charlotte's back. That was also a punishment for me.

Sometimes, I would drive out to the lake just to stare at the cabin and remember. It was a popular Airbnb, with an unparalleled view of Lake Caddo facing east toward where the lake was split between Texas and Louisiana. The cabin sat back from the lake only about ten yards, the grassy lawn sloping down toward the water line. On three sides the cabin was hidden by soaring cypress and pine trees with massive trunks and dense branch canopies.

I'd watched numerous couples pull up and rush inside with their overnight bags, eager for the promises of the night: to sit in the Adirondack chairs on the back patio, drinking wine – or bourbon, as Tom and I had — and watch the sun explode into deep burnt orange as it set in the enormous Texas sky. And then go inside, as Tom and I had.

One of those times, while daydreaming in my car across the street from the cabin, a small, white convertible pulled into the gravel driveway. I vaguely noticed the couple as if through a fog, and then, suddenly, the man's features came into focus. It was Tom. With another woman. Not my sister.

I'd texted my sister immediately.

Hey Char, just checking in. Whatcha up to tonight?

The reply came right away.

Tom is the best. He sent me off for a night at the Four Seasons so I could catch up on sleep and get a massage. Room service just came. I'm in Heaven. Call you tomorrow.

Was this their first time here? I couldn't be sure. But then I saw the way Tom's hand caressed the woman — a little scratch on the back of her neck and then a gentle swish down her back that ended with a squeeze around her waist. I'd seen him do that very same caress to my sister. He'd done it to me.

I could tell. Yes, Tom and that woman had been here before.

"This is heaven," said Charlotte as she flopped onto her back on the thick white duvet.

The setting sun shone in through the sixteenth-floor hotel window. I watched the waning beam of light slice across her eyes. She squeezed her eyes shut, long enough for the sun ray to move down to her cheeks, and then she burst into tears. I laid next to my baby sister and held her until the sun fully set.

I'd paid up for this room – a junior suite with a

sitting area, jacuzzi tub, and a little balcony that over-looked the pool. We were technically there for the seminar on grief that some new friend of Charlotte's told her about. The whole idea made me uncomfortable, but Charlotte's friend had encouraged her to come, and for some reason encouraged her to bring me for support. However, I planned to use the weekend for relaxation and to nudge her along in her journey to "move forward," as they say. The beds were plush; the beauty products were luxury. I'd booked two days of massages, facials, and body wraps. Charlotte would sleep well. The last six months had been torturous for her.

It had been six months since the accident. Time behind her... That's what she needed. I would have done anything for Charlotte before... and especially now.

I flung open the closet door and yanked two white, plush terrycloth robes off their hangers. Then I stuck my hand into the side pocket of my purse, pulled out a little jar of gummies, and shook them in Charlotte's face. "Hey, Char. What do you say to watching a comedy after dinner in our robes?"

"Yes!" she shouted. "I'm in!" There it was — a hint of excitement for the first time in months, which equated to a hint of relief for me.

While we dressed for dinner, Charlotte asked, "Abby, are you sure you're OK that I invited my new friend to join us this weekend?"

"Dinner only tonight, right? Not the... after party." I laughed. "You've been spending a lot of time with her these past few months. I'm a bit jealous. How'd you meet her again?"

"That first day I finally felt like leaving the house to walk the trail and clear my head, she happened to be on the trail. We fell in step together, and she introduced herself. She'd just moved to town, she's the same age as me, and she was looking to make friends." Charlotte shrugged. "I just sort of... sort of like the idea of having someone who wasn't involved in my life before six months ago. She's been helpful, giving me a channel to move on. She knows nothing of my life, and sometimes it feels good to leave that space."

I hoped dinner would be a quick affair so we could get back to the room and our night of comedy. I grabbed Char's hands across the table. They were warm from cradling her pre-dinner hot toddy. "Here she is!" Charlotte extracted her hands from mine and waved over to a petite woman with wavy auburn hair, wearing a little black dress that showed off the figure of a woman who for sure began all her days at the gym. The woman's face lit up when she saw Charlotte. She gave a little squeal that I heard from across the dining room. She was waving madly at Charlotte but staring straight at me with a smirk like Cruella de Vil. My forehead and the inside of my palms turned clammy before my brain even understood what was happening. I'd only seen this person from afar, so there was a chance it was mistaken identity. *Oh, please, let there be a slight chance...*

When she reached the table, Charlotte stood and wrapped her arms tight around this woman's neck, as if they'd been best friends since elementary school.

"Abby, I'd like to introduce you to Brie. Brie, this is my big sister, Abby."

* * *

It had taken two months, but I'd finally caught Tom and the woman heading to the cabin again. Charlotte had invited me over to make dinner and watch a chick flick. "There's a huge storm coming; they say maybe even a tornado. Tom took the baby to his mother's tonight, so you can crash here too if you want," she said.

Red flag. Tom was going to take the baby to his mother's but not stay there himself. I knew it.

I begged off the invitation, which I hated to do, saying I was tired. Charlotte had been disappointed, but I over-exaggerated my excitement for her getting a good night's sleep without waking up with a hangover, which was a given if I went over.

I waited in the parking lot of a gas station where I knew Tom and the woman would have to pass on their way to the cabin. They drove by in her little white car just as it got dark. I tailed at a decent distance down the empty country roads. The rain was still coming down in a fury; the dirt road leading to the cabin was nothing more than a river of mud.

I parked about fifty yards before the cabin and walked through the trees to spy on them. The storm quickly rendered my raincoat and rain boots moot — my black jeans and black sweater were drenched within seconds. I had a view of the cabin from the side, able to see both the front and back porches. The dark wood cabin was visible only as a shadow through the downpour. The wind bent the trees down to touch the cabin roof, and the waves of the lake had risen to lap onto the steps of the porch, obliterating all demarcations of a structure.

Then, only moments after they'd gone inside, I saw a streak of light from the front door and a mirage of movement through the rain. A few seconds later, there was another shot of light as the woman's car door opened. Through the howling of the wind, I couldn't hear the door slam or the car engine roar to life, but as soon as the headlights went on, I ran back to my car.

I thought about busting into the cabin and confronting Tom, but the woman was on the move, and this was my chance.

* * *

When we returned to the hotel room, I noticed Charlotte's bed still had the imprint from where the two of us had huddled together before dinner. My bed was intact.

"I'm going to take a quick shower," said Charlotte. "Mind if I go first?" I didn't mind. I needed a hot shower too, and a massage, but that would have to wait.

While she was in the bathroom, I put on the plush hotel robe and slippers. I couldn't wait to slip into the cool sheets. I picked up the weekend's seminar agenda that was sitting on Charlotte's open suitcase. There were meetings and discussion groups back-to-back on topics like "Facing Denial," "Resetting Goals," and "Releasing Anger and Blame." The next forty-eight hours would be endless.

Charlotte emerged from the bathroom in a terrycloth robe and said, "Hurry up! I'm eager to get to it!"

I was already naked with the shower running when Charlotte let out a shriek — like the one in the hospital when she'd gotten the news. I ran out with my towel half-ass covering my body.

Charlotte stood, shaking, at the top of my bed by the nightstand. Her face was frozen, her mouth open in agony and her eyes wide. Our beds were each stacked with four pillows, two by two. As was Charlotte's habit in hotel rooms to want everyone to be comfortable, she'd thrown aside *my* front pillow to ready my bed before we snuggled in for the movie.

There, on the bright white sheet, was a black pistol.

I lost my breath, not only because there was a gun under my hotel pillow, but also just for the sheer fact that there was *anything* underneath my hotel pillow. And it wasn't just any gun, I knew.

"Don't touch it!" I yelled. "Stand back!"

"Wha... what is this? My God. Whose is this?" Charlotte cried. "I just... I just moved the top pillow to the side, and it was just *here*! Some... someone left their gun!"

She was too hysterical to focus, to put two and two together, although I don't know that she would have recognized Tom's gun anyway. I did. One night I'd asked him all about it. It was just a regular, run-of-the-mill Glock 19M pistol – standard issue with FBI agents, easy to conceal. Even though I'd held that gun before, I was scared to touch it now.

Keep your cool, Abby. I grabbed the plastic laundry bag from the closet, delicately picked up the gun, and turned the bag inside-out. I threw on clothes and said, "I'll take it downstairs."

I took the stairs down sixteen flights, mumbling the entire time, berating myself for not seeing this coming, and trying to figure out *how* it had happened. Instead of taking it to the hotel manager, I stashed the gun in the trunk of my car.

Back in the room, I looked over to Charlotte, still so broken and frail. She was crouched on the seat of the desk chair, her legs pulled up tight, as if she was trying to avoid mice scurrying about the room. "What did the manager say? Has this gun been here all along? Before we checked into the room? Was it left by the previous person?" She put her hands on her head. "Oh gross – that would mean housekeeping didn't change the sheets and remake the bed."

"It's all OK, Char," I said. "The manager apologized profusely. He's going to check into it. Likely the guy who just checked out left it behind, probably his legal gun, and didn't use my bed. Why in the hell he stashed it under a pillow we'll never know."

"That's it?" asked Charlotte. "They don't need to come check the room? To see if there's anything else suspicious? Did he offer to switch us to another room?"

All good logical questions and steps that absolutely a hotel manager would have taken. *Shit.* But I knew how to manipulate my little sister. "He did. He did offer to move rooms, but they don't have any more suites, so instead he offered each of us an extra spa service this weekend. At that Charlotte perked up. *Damn* – now I needed to cough up another few hundred dollars for two more spa services.

I reminded her of my gummies and calmed her down like I had dozens of times over the past six months. We watched our favorite comfort movie – *The First Wives Club* — together on her bed. Charlotte's grief had become predictable to me, as had the ways to soothe her.

An hour into the movie, there was a light, triple knock at the door that, in our current state of mind, made us scream. "Turn down service," a woman said from the other side of the door.

"GO AWAY," we both hollered. Charlotte for sure figured that was housekeeping. I felt it could have been someone else.

Charlotte had high hopes for this weekend, as did I. But for wildly different reasons. She wanted to find a way to climb out of her grief and begin to heal, and I wanted her to forget about everything completely. Drifting off to sleep, she looked so diminished underneath the covers. "Good night," she said. I gave her two loving pats on the head in response. She closed her eyes and was out with a smile still on her face – the first genuine one I'd seen in months.

I knew for certain that was Tom's gun, and now I knew for certain who Brie was. Had she stolen a key from housekeeping? If so, could she walk into the room at any time? I stared at the connecting door. Was that Brie's room? I got up to check the lock, and then I pulled the desk chair in front of the door, jamming the back of the chair underneath the door handle.

My insides were wound to the breaking point. My legs twitched, and within seconds it felt as if my sheets were soaked in sweat. I got up and took an Ambien, knowing without it I would never be able to sleep.

* * *

I followed the little white car without my headlights on, driving blind with my eyes wide open. Even when it wasn't storming, this road at night was pitch black; the soaring trees blocked the moon and stars. I could only know the twists and turns of the road from the two pinpricks of red taillights.

I said aloud, for justification of the whole thing, "What's so urgent that this bitch had to go out in a storm? Probably to get more liquor. Or condoms." And then, "I wonder what sweet Hubby would say if it were me who returned to the cabin instead?"

I sped up, my tires sliding on the road that, although paved, was now awash with mud flowing in from the forest on both sides. If only I could catch her in a turn... A zap of lightning shot through my mind, like a *zzzt* from an old television that had gone off the air for the night. I tightened my seatbelt and pressed the gas.

I couldn't honestly say if it was the impact of my car on her bumper or the slick, muddy road that caused the little white car to careen to the side and ricochet like a pinball between the sturdy trunks of the cypress trees. When I slammed on my brakes, all I remember is a long, sideways skid for what felt like ten seconds. I tried to turn into the skid like we'd been taught in driving school, but the road was the one in charge.

Her car came to a stop with the front wrapped around an enormous tree trunk, and the impact must have caused a massive limb to drop on the top of the car. The driver's side was crushed in, and smoke escaped out of the mangled hood while the headlights shone onto gnarled branches that hung from the thick copse of trees. A weak interior light flickered from one of the passenger side doors that had flung open. I could make out just the top of a head over the driver's seat.

Nobody would ever doubt that the storm had caused such an awful accident. I jumped out of my car to make sure the bitch was dead.

Charlotte and I ran into Brie at the breakfast buffet. Charlotte was nice and rested; I'd tossed and turned despite the Ambien. Charlotte filled her plate before I did, and by the time I got to the table, she was full-on into telling Brie about the gun under my pillow. After she mentioned to Brie that I'd brought it to the manager, Brie caught my eye and said, "Smart thinking. It could have been used in a murder for all we know."

Charlotte finished quickly and announced she was off to a morning discussion group about anger, and we planned to meet for our facials at eleven. As soon as Charlotte disappeared, Brie said, "I have something for you."

She slid what used to be a bright pink eyeglasses

case onto the table. It was covered in dried mud. I inhaled, and a large piece of pancake flew down the wrong pipe. My coughing and gagging caught the attention of the entire dining room. Brie sat patiently waiting for me to finish.

"Been missing this?" Brie asked. Her voice was a low rumble. A wave of nausea ran through my gut. "I'm sure you were long-gone by the time I got there. After a half hour, and Tom not answering his phone, I ran down the road to find him. Where *you* left him. All alone. I couldn't miss the bright pink case sticking out of the mud. It was the only piece of color in that whole scene amid the brown and dark red blood. Looks like you have expensive glasses, so it was a good idea to put your name and phone number on the inside. Thought I'd stash it away after I called 911, before the cops had the chance to see it. So... you're welcome."

She taunted me with the case, wagging it in front of me. I grabbed it and stuffed it in my purse. "What the hell? You have no idea what you're—"

"Zip it, Abby. I'm not an idiot. The cause of death was 'blunt force trauma,' but the autopsy report said the gash on his forehead was 'inconsistent' with hitting his head on the windshield. What they told Charlotte, which I'm sure you're aware of, is that he must have hit his head on something and then gotten in the car. They are assuming he was driving to the hospital for help, and the blood loss made him dizzy, causing him to crash. You are aware that is the current line of thinking with the police, right?"

I just stared at Brie, trying to mask my fear with confidence I didn't quite have at the moment.

Brie turned her chair sideways. I dropped my head to look down. She took her right index finger, placed it under my chin, and flipped my head up so I was forced to look her in the eyes. In the process, her fingernail left a papercut-like scrape. Brie emphasized her last word. "*Right*, Abby?"

I wanted to scream at her with all my being, but the ball in my throat prevented me from opening my mouth. Instead, the urge betrayed me and came out as thick tears.

Brie smiled and kept going. "I wonder..." she scratched her chin and then wiggled her fingers, "if I'd turned in the gun, would the authorities have been able to match it with the gash on Tom's head? And if I happened to anonymously turn in your eyeglass case, that would sure be a big help toward solving how he died, and perhaps in solving what caused the crash. If it wasn't an accident, that is."

After what seemed like an eternity, I saw the driver's door open just a crack. I trudged into the tree line through a foot of muck to reach the car. The rain was like tiny marbles pelleting my face – it was coming down too hard for even the dense tree canopy to slow it down. My hands were constant windshield wipers keeping my hair out of my eyes. It felt as if my raincoat weighed a hundred pounds.

I stood paralyzed, in shock but in sordid awe at the scene in front of me. Then all at once, the door was flung open.

It wasn't her.

Half of Tom's body fell onto the ground; the other half still strained against his seat belt. I fell to my knees in solidarity. He looked at me. Or he looked in my direction – the blood on his face surely clouded his vision. My heart constricted as I raced to him, but everything was in slow motion – either from me having to slog through the thick mud, or the unbelievability of the moment that I was looking at Tom and not the woman, or both.

He tried to get his full body out, but his right leg seemed to be twisted behind him – almost as if it was still on the gas pedal. His right arm looked to be reaching down in an attempt to free his right foot. I watched him from my frozen position no more than ten feet away as he moved his left arm in slow motion across his body. I was almost rooting for him to succeed. Or... maybe not. I knew he kept his gun in a pocket of his cargo pants on the right side – something I'd discovered our first night together when we'd playfully rolled down the grass hill that led from the back of the cabin to the lake. Was that what he was reaching for? Did he know I had caused the crash?

He contorted, I thought to try and reach the gun that way, but he couldn't get to it. I let out my breath.

Then the *click* of the seatbelt somehow made it through the wind and whipping rain, knocking me out of my trance and forcing me into action. That's what he'd been reaching for. I didn't know if he'd seen me yet, but I couldn't let him get to that gun.

* * *

I cancelled my morning massage and spent the time sitting outside Charlotte's meeting room, in case Brie might try and slink in there. Had Brie mentioned anything to Charlotte in their short friendship? Something that could throw doubt on the accident? Charlotte's meeting ended at ten-thirty, and then she was supposed to meet me for our facials. I couldn't take the chance she'd run up to the room or be alone at any point. Charlotte would open the door without hesitation for Brie.

Lunch was another tense encounter between Brie and me, but luckily the airtime was taken up by Charlotte who had lots to say about her morning session with her new fellow widows. Brie seemed intent on peppering Charlotte with questions about her anger and blame. Charlotte said, "Actually, this afternoon there's a group discussion on 'releasing blame,' or something like that. I don't know who I'd blame, other than Mother Nature, but I'm game to try anything." Charlotte shrugged, and I shivered.

I didn't want to spend my afternoon on a hard bench in the hotel lobby, so I gave in and headed toward the spa. The deep tissue massage did nothing to relieve the tension in my shoulders. Despite the instrumental music and heated table, my mind raced in circles. I was not only still full of knots when it was finished, but also, I was sure I'd be bruised from the masseuse's tough fingers. I still had forty-five minutes before meeting Charlotte back in the room, so I thought I might as well spend fifteen of it in the steam room. I had a lot to sweat out.

The steam was on full blast when I entered. I walked into a wall of wet and stuck my hands out to find a seat. Just as I settled onto a bench, leaned back against the slick wall, and let my towel droop open, she spoke, low and deep. "You know I'm not here by accident."

Despite the humidity, goosebumps broke out up and down my arms. "Br... Brie?" I heard the swish of a wet towel and the squeak of feet sliding into flip flops, and then the apparition of a body appeared right in front of me.

Two white orbs shone through the mist. "Seems we've got this all to ourselves."

"This isn't a coincidence. Stay away from my sister."

"I'm not going to hurt your sister, dear Abby. If she knew the truth, she'd know that she and I are on the same team. Against you. Did you enjoy your little surprise?"

"You know Charlotte found the gun instead of me. How did you know which bed was mine?"

"Lovers talk." Brie shrugged. "Tom said Char always liked the side of the bed in hotels by the window. I took a gamble. It didn't pay off like I expected, but I'm OK with Char being a bit on edge."

"You may NOT use her nickname."

Brie waved my comment away. "All the same to me. So, Abby... what shall we do about your little predicament?"

"Nothing, Brie. It's over. Charlotte doesn't need to know about you and Tom. Let her heal."

"I know you were in love with him too, so cut the bullshit because that's not an option. There's just one way this is going to go, but there are two options on how we get there." The steam came back on full blast, sounding like a screeching tea kettle — like Brie's voice. "Option One: You will break Charlotte's heart and tell her Tom had been having an affair with me since she was pregnant; you will tell her we were in love; and then you will convince her to give me a million dollars from Tom's inheritance that was bequeathed to sweet Charlotte."

"That's absurd. Tom doesn't have that kind of money. I'm not listening to this." I stood and turned toward the door, to leave the claustrophobia of the steam room.

Brie's hands clamped down on my shoulders, and she stuck her face right in mine. "Awww... *perhaps* Tom wasn't as into you as you thought with your little affair? *Perhaps* he didn't share with you about his inheritance from his grandparents? *Perhaps* your sweet sister doesn't tell you everything?" Each "perhaps" got louder and louder. I backed up until the bench hit the back of my knees.

"And if you don't believe me, then *perhaps* you should SIT BACK DOWN and hear your second option." She slammed me down on the bench. The slick wood caused me to slide forward and bang my tailbone on the edge. "As I was saying before you interrupted... Option Two: I tell Charlotte about *your* little tryst with Tom and fill in some of the blanks for her about the accident. In option one, she loses some money and her faith in her late husband but keeps her relationship with her older sister intact. In option two, she loses respect for you and goes off the deep end knowing that her only source of support has betrayed her."

Once again, the outline of Brie's body emerged from the falling mist. It seemed to loom larger than before. I needed to get out of the steam room before I passed out.

"And I can't quite figure out how, but Charlotte

knew about us, Tom and me," Brie said. "Or should I say she knew of me, but not exactly who I was. She's not the innocent lamb you make her out to be. She'd been sending me threatening texts before the accident."

I stood up again and fought against the head rush. "Let me rephrase," Brie said. "Charlotte knew that Tom was having an affair, but she didn't know he was having *two* affairs. I know what you did, and I will NOT hesitate to throw you under the bus if I don't get what I want. What I deserve. I gave that man a year of myself, and he *owed* me."

I tried to change the subject. "So, you gave us back his pistol?"

Brie sneered. "I'm not stupid, Abby. I grew up around guns. I removed the hammer, so it won't shoot anymore." She opened the door to the steam room, letting the cold locker-room air rush in. "Although, you seemed to manage turning it into a murder weapon without taking a shot."

It took me five leaps through the mud to reach Tom and the car, the rainwater and mud spilling over the rims of my rain boots. I banged my shin hard along the way, a moment I didn't register at the time but two days later would come back with a vengeance as a massive hematoma.

I threw myself across his body, and he let out a noise that was half-groan and half-growl. I yanked at the Velcro pocket of his cargo pants and grabbed the gun. Then I crab-walked backwards, leaving a safe distance between us. Tom ignored me and the gun. He didn't care that I had it. He might not even have noticed that I had it. That's when it hit me – he hadn't been reaching for his gun. He'd just been trying to get out of the damn seat belt.

He stared at me from his position on all fours, surely not comprehending, and probably not believing, that I was there, a spectator to the horror show. He turned and crawled through the mud and the tree roots to the back door of the car, which seemed to still be intact. He yanked on the door. At first, it wouldn't budge, and I took a step forward to help him, but my brain must have been ten steps ahead and stopped me just as Tom managed to open the door and reach inside.

I'd never seen Tom hurt, physically or emotionally. He was FBI, ex-military, a rock. With his right leg completely disengaged from his body, he turned around. Despite the driving rain and my black raincoat with the hood drawstring pulled tight around my face, and despite the blood dripping into his eyes, I knew then that Tom knew it was me. It was as if a switch had flipped. Holding something in his left arm, with his right he reached into his pants pocket for the gun, only then registering that I had it.

How would I explain this? The sheer fact I was there, at the accident, deep in the woods? I couldn't call 911. Tom's head drooped – I think he realized that I wasn't going to make that call. Instead, I threw my arms around him, and the two of us rocked together in the mud as the rain subsided. He didn't ask why I was there. After many minutes, he passed out.

I knew what I had to do. It was obvious. Simple and easy. I'd never pointed a gun at anyone, loaded or unloaded. I didn't trust myself. If I shot Tom, there would be an investigation. I looked around. Except for the break in the tree canopy, I couldn't see where the road ended and the forest began. Rivers of mud ran everywhere. No shoe prints. It was only then I realized I'd luckily been wearing my winter gloves the whole time.

I made a split-second decision to change course, and I'll never, ever be able to explain the craze that came over me. All I could focus on was the fact that Tom was, eventually, going to wake up or be found. That couldn't happen. I held the gun tight in my right hand. I knew I had only one attempt. Two would look suspicious. I moved away the few hairs from Tom's face that were covering his left temple, as if those hairs would prevent the blow from achieving maximum impact. And then I brought the gun down with a thud.

* * *

I didn't like Brie's Option One or Option Two, so I decided to go with Option Three.

We were leaving early the next morning. It had to be tonight. While Charlotte was in the shower, I grabbed her phone and typed in the password only a sister would know. I knew Brie's number by heart – I'd plucked it from Tom's phone one night when I'd gone to dinner with him and Charlotte. I punched in the numbers and noticed it now popped up in Charlotte's contacts. My fingers flew over the keys as I typed: I KNOW WHO YOU ARE, AND I KNOW WHAT MY SISTER'S DONE. I'LL NEVER BE ABLE TO FORGIVE HER, BUT I'LL FORGIVE YOU IF YOU HELP ME FINISH THIS. I'LL GIVE YOU ANYTHING YOU WANT. MEET ME IN THE STEAM ROOM TONIGHT AT 11 PM.

And then I deleted it.

I was already there, in the back corner of the steam room, when Brie arrived. "Take a seat," I said, in my perfect imitation of my sister's voice. I had one towel wrapped around my body and one around my hair, and I knew through the steam I could be a dead ringer for Charlotte.

"Thank you, Brie, for encouraging me to come this weekend. If there's one thing I've learned, it's how to deal with my anger," I said. "I need to ask myself, 'Is my anger valid?' Who, exactly, am I angry at? I can't be angry at a car accident, can I? That's as logical as being angry at Mother Nature for making the storm in the first place. Could I be angry at Tom for having an affair? Sure, but that doesn't provide me with an outlet right now. So, the only thing that comes to mind is to be angry at the *reason* he was out at that cabin and on the road that night in the first place. And that brings me to you."

"And to your sister," said Brie.

"And to my sister," I said. "Which is perhaps the worst of all. So, I have a plan, and if you help me out here, I'll make it worth your while. I know you know about Tom's trust fund."

"What do you need from me?" asked Brie. "I'll do it and then take that money and disappear."

The steam started up, filling the room once again and rendering us invisible to each other. I pulled out the gun and walked the four paces I'd measured out toward Brie, then with one blow, the grip of the pistol connected with her left temple. It was a smooth execution... I'd done it before.

Two murders: one a husband who was straying and whose trust fund would support his wife for the rest of her life, and the other the woman who he was having an affair with and who'd blackmailed her sister for a huge portion of that money.

Charlotte would be forgiven, eventually. Most would certainly understand the extreme emotional toll something like this would take on a young widow. I left the gun next to Brie's body and Charlotte's phone on the bench. Even though I'd deleted all her text messages with Brie, I knew phone history was recoverable. Then I removed my thin, blue gloves. I'd flush them down the toilet later.

There was a visible difference between a passed-out Tom and a dead Tom. I knew it from the way his body slumped. Strangely, the rain seemed to have stopped at the precise moment Tom's heart did too. I heard, in the midnight quiet, the air leaving his lungs. And then I gently – as if that would matter – placed the gun back in Tom's cargo pants pocket.

I couldn't leave the scene without dealing with the car. The airbags had exploded, but the windshield was shattered. An enormous branch had swung down and hit it from the outside. I risked remaining there for a bit longer and heaved the branch off the front of the car. Now it would look like Tom's head had done that damage.

I still shudder when I remember watching Tom as he struggled with the back door. He hadn't called to me for help, likely because he was still in disbelief that I was there. That anyone was there. He'd finally gotten the back door flung open. In horror, I'd watched as Tom pulled at a car seat. *A car seat?* That little hussy didn't have a kid. I'd stalked her long enough to know that. His movements were frantic. His body shielded me from seeing what he was doing, and then he turned and fell against the car. His mouth opened to a wail that was swallowed up by the storm. But I'd heard it loud and clear.

Someone else would find them and call 911. Easily explained — a dark and stormy night, a father and son out for a drive, an unfortunate accident. The police hadn't been notified of the crash until the next morning when a woman drove by the wreckage. I was with Charlotte in the hospital when they'd brought in the bodies, but she went alone to the police station to make a statement, where she told them, truthfully, that she'd had no idea why her husband and son were in the area of Lake Caddo the previous night.

For the past six months, I'd comforted my sister as best as anyone could comfort someone while holding a knife and stabbing them in the back.

I couldn't shake the image of Tom turning around to face me that night, his face contorted with unimaginable pain. Did he see my pain too? Did he understand what I was going through?

Anyone who knew Tom wouldn't be surprised that he'd survived a massive head wound long enough to reach into that back seat. I hadn't understood at first. But then I saw it – the blue-and-white checkered blanket that my nephew never, ever went anywhere without. The one his Aunt Abby had given him the day he was born.

I left my nephew in Tom's arms while I killed him with his own gun – it was the least I could do.

From the Author

This story came from a weekend trip to Dallas when my husband found a gun under his hotel pillow as he was flipping it over to take a nap. While he and my son stood in disbelief, my brain immediately went off in all sorts of juicy directions—who could have planted it, what kinds of crimes has it been involved in, and should we lie in wait for the perp to come back and retrieve it? Guess that's just the kind of writer I'm meant to be.

When I'm not writing about not-nice things, I think I'm a pretty nice person... unless I'm on the soccer field. You can find me in Austin, Texas, likely rooting for the Longhorns at a Tex-Mex restaurant.

If you'd like to read another not-nice story, look for my short story, *Bloodline*.

Deadly Evidence
Sonja Dewing

Prologue: The Third Victim

I blinked awake, unsure why my eyes were open before dawn. Had I heard that rustling, or was it just part of a dream? Reluctantly, I reached up and tapped the light, squinting against the sudden brightness. The bed was warm and inviting, but that faint sound gnawed at my thoughts. I couldn't shake the feeling that I should check the house.

My habit of tossing and turning had left my covers in a mess, and I had even managed to untuck the blanket and the sheet. I started moving the covers out of the way then realized my legs didn't want to move. Actually, they *couldn't* move. Concerned, I tossed the sheet aside.

I stared in disbelief at my shriveled legs and feet. Below the knees, they looked like sand, pitted and folded in barely the shape of legs.

Strangely, there was no pain.

Sweat beaded on my forehead.

Then I noticed a glow all over my legs, tiny pulses of light that seemed to match the beat of my heart.

Quickly, I realized I had to be dreaming.

"Get it together, Jackie," I said to myself. Nothing else could explain this bizarre sight. I took a deep breath and tried to calm myself. Since I couldn't seem to wake up, I examined my nightmare.

Upon closer inspection of my lower legs, I could see a thin, wispy web. The threads crisscrossed around each of my toes and over my legs. In some places the threads were dense. I noticed a part of my right thigh was beginning to change and watched horrified to see my skin collapse. Then it dawned on me that I could *feel* something moving in my thigh. Maybe this was not just a nightmare.

I began reciting a mantra, "Wake up, wake up." It wasn't working. This couldn't be real. There was no discomfort. But if it was real, I had to get help. I reached for the phone and saw that my right hand was covered with a thin web and there was a glow in my fingers. I had to work hard just to get my right hand to grasp the receiver. Putting the receiver up to my face, I reached over to dial with my left hand and watched as my index finger crumbled away.

This was no nightmare. I realized too late that putting my hand up close to my face had not been a good idea. I could feel something swimming through my cheeks and there was a strange metallic taste in my mouth.

Mercifully, I felt myself slipping into darkness.

Sheriff Mora Gentry

I drove through my town with a sense of dread. Something was targeting my wonderful and quirky residents, and this wellness check could be another victim. But I was probably worrying for nothing. I rolled down the windows and let the cool, fall air drift through my graying blonde hair.

After parking in Jackie's driveway behind her leaf-covered car, I pulled my hair into a bun, one as tight as the knot in my stomach. If there had been someone else to send, I would have sent them.

Maybe my friend wasn't feeling well, but then why hadn't Jackie called into work? Her boss had called the sheriff's office—my office—this morning. She hadn't been to work for three days. I raised my hand to knock on her door.

"Sheriff Mora Gentry!"

I whirled around. "For God's sake, Darren! You scared the crap out of me."

"Sorry." Darren stepped back, eyes wide, and palms out. "I would never want to scare the town's top karate expert."

I rolled my eyes at him. Darren was in his standard outfit, a suit and cowboy hat with black boots. At least today, his clothes matched the oncoming fall season.

Darren pointed to his car parked on the street. "I was interviewing a local business owner, she lives up the road. I saw your car and thought I'd see why you're here."

Darren and I often saw each other at yoga and occasionally bonded over local football games, but that didn't mean he wasn't always looking for something to put in the paper. Even though it wasn't procedure to have him here, I didn't want to send him away. I didn't want to face this alone.

"I'm doing a wellness check." I turned back to the door, reluctantly.

"Could this have to do with those other two deaths? The ones you don't want to talk about?"

I sighed in response to his question and the fact that no one seemed to be coming to answer the door. "And, I'm still not going to talk about those deaths, yet."

Darren walked up to the living room window and looked in. "I don't see anyone. Have they been missing work?"

"Darren, stop tramping in the grass. If there's any foul play here, I'll need to examine everything."

He nodded at me. "So, there *is* something going on. Come on, you can tell me. I can promise to keep it out of the paper, at least for a little while."

I'd have to give Darren some information. If Jackie were dead, the idea made me gag a little — and if she was a pile of bones like the others, it was time to get the word out. Maybe the townspeople could keep themselves safe until I could find the reason behind these mysterious deaths.

"Darren, follow me closely. Don't touch anything."

I knew the moment I walked in that something was wrong. It was that same smell I had noticed in the other two locations. I blinked back tears for my friend.

"What does that smell like to you?" I asked Darren.

"Like, cologne or rubbing alcohol? Or both?"

I nodded, "I think you're right. There's also a bit of something else. Desiccation? Does that have a smell?"

"You mean, like a dead body? Nah, I've smelled a dead body before, a few years back at the morgue. It's not like this."

I wished he was right, but I knew better. "Well, you've never seen a dead body like the ones I've been seeing."

We walked into the bedroom and there was Jackie, or at least what was left of her. Her bones, an odd blueish color, were laid out on her side, one arm stretched towards the phone. Her flesh was gone. Her empty sockets seemed to be staring at us.

"Holy shit!" Darren stepped back and fell over his own feet.

Tears came to my eyes, but I took a deep breath and

blinked them away. I turned from the scene and helped him up. I had to do my job but my voice broke just a little. "I have to search the house for any evidence."

Darren's eyes were wide. "The other two deaths that you don't want to talk about, is this how they looked?"

I nodded. "Yes. Nothing but bones and any clothes that they were last seen wearing."

"They're not fake bones?"

"I wish. There were three dogs found before it started with humans. They looked the same, that blue color, and all real."

He peered around me into the room. "I need to get closer for some pictures."

I grasped his shoulders, focusing on his face and trying to keep at bay the memories of barbecues and birthdays in this house with my friend, but not being successful. "Darren, I'm the only sheriff, I have no staff, I have no forensic expert. I can't let you closer. I have to go over this house with a fine-tooth comb. However, I don't want to be alone. Can you put your newspaper aside for a little while and just keep me company?"

He glanced at the bed and then at me, it finally dawning on him. "Oh shit. This is Jackie's house. Damn, I'm sorry."

I nodded at him. "Follow me out. I need to mark off the house from anyone entering."

"Mora, shouldn't you call someone to help?"

I scoffed. "Who should I call? My deputy quit two

weeks ago to take a job in Chicago. Luckily, I'm a certified crime scene investigator. I know what to collect. I called the FBI the day I found the first set of human bones and asked them to send me a forensic specialist to analyze everything."

Darren backed up in the hallway. "I know some people that might be able to help. I've interviewed some specialists for newspaper articles, a few of them live in that new housing development right outside town with the million-dollar houses."

I knew the one, the houses were so big you could fit a family of twenty just in the living room.

"What kind of specialists?" I asked.

"Oh, well, there's this lady that does data analysis for some lab and then I think there was a forensic guy. He's an inventor but also works as a consultant for a big company. And a couple of other scientist types that might have some forensic skills."

I nodded and led Darren out to the front yard so I could grab the police tape from the car. "Write down their info for me. I'll contact them to see what they can do."

* * *

Hours later, with the car door open, I sat in the passenger side of my car for a break. Darren handed me a cup of coffee from the only coffee shop in town. I breathed in the smell of the sugary latte. "Thank you, Darren."

He nodded toward the house. "Can I get in to take photos?"

I shook my head. "I appreciate you hanging around, but we don't know what killed Jackie. I'm going through the bedroom dressed in my protective gear. The doorway is as far as I could ever let you in."

"Tell you what, I'll send you photos and information, not just from this scene, but from the others as well. There are some things I don't want the public to know, not yet."

I expected him to argue, but he nodded instead. "You've been really thorough. I think part two of my article will be how hard our sheriff works."

He turned to go. "I know you've had a hard day, but the sooner you can send the information to me, the better." Then he walked away.

I sipped the hot coffee, thankful that Berdie kept her little specialty coffee shop open until the afternoon. And then I remembered that day Jackie and I had sat at the picnic tables outside the coffee shop, just last week. We had talked about our newfound love of kickboxing.

Jackie had asked me, "No more karate?"

I had nodded. "I've reached the highest point I can, nowhere else to go. I need a new challenge."

She had laughed, "Another mountain to climb? At fifty-four?"

"Look who's talking. You're enjoying it just as much as me and you're forty-five."

She nodded. "Us older people have to stick together and show those young kids how it's done."

And now Jackie had no more time to spend anywhere. It was such a waste.

I let the tears come as I punched at the dashboard. No matter what, I was going to find out what was going on and put a stop to it.

It was time to pack every piece of evidence in the house out to the car. I had taken so many photos of the bones, of what was left of Jackie. Now, what was left to do was to put her, piece by piece, into an evidence bag.

I wished Darren had hung around, but I also knew that if I didn't get the photos and some text to him soon, he'd publish everything he knew, which wasn't ideal.

As I put on a new set of protective gear and another set of purple industrial gloves, I hoped Jackie wouldn't mind. She had never been a fan of purple. Then it hit me, the kitchen.

I went back to the kitchen and straight for the small purple storage container that sat on the kitchen counter. I hadn't thought anything about it before, but it was sitting in the middle of the counter and had seemed out of place from what I knew of Jackie. Had there been one of these at the other crime scenes? I couldn't remember any, but maybe it was something. I bagged it with the other evidence and headed for the worst job of all.

On the bed, there was no skin or dust, but hovering over the bones made me uncomfortable. I started with her foot bones so I wouldn't have to look at her skull until last. As I picked up the first bone, through the gloves they felt cold and solid, like they had never been part of a warm, human body.

Unfortunately, when I got to her shoulders, her skull rolled down the pillow onto the bed.

I stepped back and closed my eyes, speaking to Jackie on the off chance she could hear me from wherever she was now. "Oh man, Jackie, I'm so sorry. You should be here to go play with your nephews or make that Memphis rub for the upcoming Labor Day picnic."

I stepped up to the bed, gingerly picked up the skull, and set it in the bag. Then I bagged the pillow and the sheets.

With what was left of my dear friend, I headed for the office.

After storing the evidence, I took a long hot shower. That and the washer/dryer were the few necessary amenities I had added to the office last year. I changed into workout clothes and checked my uniform which was currently in the sanitary cycle of the washer.

I waited to call Jackie's sister until I knew she'd be home from work and kept the details to a minimum.

After that, yet another emotionally draining moment, I knew I had to feed my own body and soul. That was the benefit of being older and wiser, or maybe just older.

I didn't want to take a class today, didn't want to have to explain why Jackie wasn't there, so I went to one of the punching bags and started. Jab cross, kick, upper-cut, kick. Rhythm and focus helped me escape the stress for a little while. I left the gym feeling strong and hungry.

Steve, my lazy little pug, greeted me at the door with his tail wagging. My heart felt lighter as I swooped him up and took him with me to the couch.

Sure, I'd rather have a golden retriever or a Bernese mountain dog, but last month I had been walking in the park near my house when I saw someone set Steve on the side of the road and take off in their moving truck.

Did they think that a pug was going to forage in the park? Or maybe get in touch with its wolf DNA hidden somewhere very, very, very deep? Well, they didn't deserve this squishy love bug.

He flopped down in my lap and fell asleep almost instantly, snoring of course. Normally, I'd be stuck, not wanting to wake him. "Sorry little dude, I need dinner."

As soon as I set him on the floor, he went through the dog door into the backyard while I went to the kitchen and prepped dinner. I could see through the kitchen window that the new underground electric fence was doing its job, keeping him from leaving the unfenced yard that abutted the park.

As my chicken cooked on the stove, he came running back in as fast as his little legs could carry him, then used his sad puppy eyes on me.

"Oh, Steve." I gave him his dinner and even though I had no intention of giving him my food, I tossed in a couple pieces of chicken. I know, I'm a softy.

I took my dinner and a small glass of wine into the backyard. The sun was setting and I pulled my sweater closer against the breeze.

I'd make it a point to hang out with friends soon, but for today, this was at least a nice ending to a terrible day. Meanwhile, I hoped the FBI forensic examiner would get here soon. I had heard good and bad about FBI personnel. Would they give their best to help solve the mystery, or was I about to embark on a hard-fought journey to get the information I needed?

FBI Mobile Lab

Bright and early, I got to the office. Getting out of my car, a young man approached me. He wore a light grey sweater and dark green khakis. He looked like he had stepped right off of a college campus.

"Sheriff Gentry? I heard you need a deputy."

I stopped in my tracks. "Deputy?" Either young people were getting younger, or I was getting really old. "I've never even seen you around town, what makes you think you'd be a good deputy?" I asked him.

Just then, a long grey vehicle pulled into the parking lot. I thought maybe a food truck had gotten lost. Before he could answer, a mocha-skinned woman got out of the truck and approached me. Her black hair was pulled back and the ends splayed out like a peacock. "Sheriff Gentry?"

I nodded.

"I'm Billy Rutledge, the forensic expert you called for." She held up her credentials.

"Ms. Rutledge—"

"Call me Billy."

"Okay. Billy."

"Sheriff Mora!" A group of citizens were walking across the parking lot with Tom, the local preacher. Father Tom was always a kind soul, but along with him were the town busybody, Nora, as well as Brian Lomax, the town troublemaker. Nora was carrying her famous Jello dessert — I was pretty sure she used the rum-infused sweet to ply unknowing people into sharing gossip or other useful information.

I took a deep breath and put a smile on my face, yet thought to myself that I must have done something terrible in my past life. "Billy, feel free to meet me inside. This shouldn't take long."

Billy nodded and went into the building. I was happy to focus on at least one thing at a time.

"Sheriff Mora." Father Tom was now within earshot. "We're concerned about three important members of the town having recently died."

Brian stepped around Father Tom. "We have a right to know what's going on."

Tom reached out to put his hand on Brian's shoulder, but Brian was already in my face. Brian would take any opportunity to find fault in what I did, seeing as he had tried to get my job a few times over the years. It was his hot temper that had kept him from getting any respectable job.

But I wasn't going to let him push my buttons. I took a step back and nodded. "There's an active ongoing investigation."

Tom moved in between us and faced Brian. "Brian, we talked about this. We're going to remain civil."

I had almost forgotten about the young guy aiming for a deputy position until he stepped up next to Brian.

Brian had a grimace on his face, obviously not interested in what Tom wanted. He stepped back from Tom and tripped on a parking lot divider. His meaty arm swung out to Tom as if to try to catch himself, but it connected with the young man's face. At the same time, his other arm hit Nora's Jello pan, sending it straight up into the air.

I wanted to help Brian and the young man, but I needed to know where the Jello was going to land first. I watched it tumble through the air with a growing sense of alarm. It landed with a *splump.* The red squishy shrapnel splashed in chunks all over my uniform and a few pieces landed on my cheek. The scent of rum was soaking into my clothes.

Nora exclaimed, "Oh!"

Father Tom looked genuinely distressed at my uniform. "We should probably come back at another time."

I sighed, grabbed the pieces off of my face, and brushed off as much of the chunks from my uniform as I could. "You'll soon be getting some public information about what's happening. In the meantime, I have to get back to work."

Nora picked up the tin, leaving the goo on the ground.

I gently guided the young man, who had his hands over his face, into my office. When I knew no one was looking I plopped the two pieces from my cheek into my mouth. If this was going to be one of those days, I deserved a little red Jello.

$$* \quad * \quad *$$

I handed the young man an ice pack as he sat back in my office chair and placed it on his face. At least it covered up the bloody tissues stuffed up his nose to help stop the bleeding.

"What's your name?"

He pulled the ice pack down to look me in the eyes. "T.A. Park."

"T.A. what was your plan? Stepping in between Tom and Brian like that?"

He closed his eyes and pulled the ice pack up. "I was stepping closer so I could talk to them, use some of my de-escalation I learned in college. Like how we all want the same thing — to find answers."

The idea sounded good in theory, something I had tried in my first year as Sheriff, but some people didn't want to be calmed down. They wanted a fight. But that was something one learned.

He nodded toward Billy. "Please, Sheriff, you're busy. Don't worry about me."

I turned to Billy, feeling like a country bumpkin covered in Jello next to the FBI expert. "I'll show you the evidence room and then get changed."

"Is it always this crazy around here?" Billy asked as we walked to the back room.

I shook my head. "This town is usually the quiet,

carefree place we advertise in our tourism commercials, but in the past month it has increasingly become scary."

I led her to the back room. "Billy, how long have you been working for the FBI?"

"Three years now. Before that, I was working for the Montana Department of Justice's Forensic Science Division."

"Wow." I glanced over at Billy. "I'm impressed. I've heard a lot of great things from that crime lab."

Billy nodded. "It was hard to leave. I learned so much from my colleagues in Montana, but when I had an opportunity with the FBI, I had to take it."

"Montana though? Couldn't have been easy. I've been to Montana. Not a lot of cultural diversity."

"Definitely not. No, *I was* the cultural diversity. So, tell me what we have here."

We stopped at the end of the table. The evidence bags and paperwork were sitting in neat rows. At least I felt better about handing over the evidence to someone who had some expertise. "There have been six incidents so far, three dogs and three humans."

"Incidents?"

I shrugged. "The bodies were nothing but bones. These were animals and people who had been seen alive a few days before their bones were found. The first victims were dogs. The first human body found was—"

"No, don't tell me," Billy said. "Let me look through your reports, and get a look at the evidence. Then I'll ask you to chat with me. But there should be three sets of human bones and three sets of animal bones."

I nodded. "Everything is here on these two tables. Reports, anything I collected at the scenes, including the bones."

"No time like the present. I'll get the change of custody forms, and we'll start working on the evidence." Billy said.

I pointed out the window at the grey monstrosity. "Your truck, is that some kind of mobile lab?"

Billy smiled. "Some kind? Sheriff, it's all that and more. I was lucky. A different team was going to take it to Oklahoma, but the killer they were after was caught. I was able to commandeer it. Come on, I'll show it to you."

"Mora, you're welcome to call me Mora." I followed close behind. I had only seen one crime lab, the one back in school. Our town would never have enough money to put one together, much less a mobile one.

The lab was impressive and Billy seemed to be the type of person who would collaborate, hopefully. As I exited the lab, T.A. was standing outside, the ice and bloody tissues gone. He had the great beginnings of a black eye.

"Hey, Sheriff. I get it if you don't need any help. I didn't make the best first impression."

But, he had taken initiative and sometimes that's what this job needed. "I'll get you to fill out some paperwork and take you on as an intern."

He grinned. "Fire!"

I nodded. "Fire." Great, I was going to have to learn all the young kid lingo. I led him into the office. "You can start by filling out this paperwork." I motioned him towards my desk. "Then you can move the evidence into the lab."

As he sat down to fill out his job application, he also handed me his card, "T.A. Park, College Student." It included his Instagram handle, BasketballandCriminalJustice.

It was certainly better than other handles I had seen.

I filed his paperwork and then watched him grab a box of evidence bags and take them across the parking lot. I waited until he had stepped into the lab — just to make sure he wasn't some fake who was here to run away with evidence.

Then I finally had a chance to change clothes. I presoaked the red splotches, hoping that the red dye would come out. Maybe I could outlaw Nora's Jello or the rum or both.

When I sat at my desk, Darren's note was the first thing I noticed. He had given me the names of his experts. With the help from the FBI, I didn't need to talk to them. Plus, all I could think about when I pictured that fancy development in the hills was that things had been quiet and peaceful up until those big houses were built.

I tossed the note in the trash.

If only Billy could help me figure this whole thing out before another person was struck dead. But I had a feeling, it wasn't going to be that easy.

Deadly Evidence

After seeing the sheriff out of my lab, I put on my protective gear. I didn't envy the sheriff, having these grizzly deaths and not much information. But I was here to change that.

I opened the box marked 1A and looked through the file.

The paperwork named the bones in the bags as Astral Ryan, thirty-five years old. Her bones had been found in her living room, lying on a yoga mat. Her yoga clothes had been on her body — all of the clothing had been synthetic material — spandex, etc.

I set the bag of clothing aside and started on the bags of bones. If I didn't know any better, I would have thought these were from someone who had died years ago. And the strange blue color made them look like they had been bought at a Halloween store. But the weight and the feel of them in my gloved hand told me these were real enough.

I gingerly removed one bone after another, setting it

in anatomical placement on the table until everything was set.

The door opening made me jump. It was the kid with a box, he was staring at the bones.

"Woah."

"You can set the boxes along the wall over on the far side, Kid."

"The name's T.A."

"Right, T.A."

He dropped the box and came back to look, peering closely at the bones of the left hand. "Wow. Was this the first victim?"

"Yes, but you should step back, I don't want you this close without protective-" I noticed a spot of blood drip from T.A.'s nose onto a hand bone. "Damn it, T.A. Step back. You're bleeding on the bones."

T.A. jumped back and stopped the drips with his hand. "Oh shit, I'm sorry! That hit to the nose was hard."

I walked over to the other side of the table and reached down with a towel to clean up the blood, but it was gone. "Maybe you didn't drip."

"No, I did. I'm sorry. It's right..." He paused to look in the same location. "I saw it. It was there."

The hairs on my arms raised. "Get out. Shut the door behind you. I'll be in here for a few hours, maybe more."

T.A. backed up to the door.

I realized I needed to try and repeat the incident. "No wait. If you're still bleeding, put some drops in one of those petri dishes before you leave."

He did just that, letting a few drops fall, then set the dish on the counter near the door. He stepped out and shut the door.

I took the dish with blood and reached far over the table, keeping myself as far up and away as possible. A drop landed an inch away from the hand bones. It remained.

Then I let a drip land on the same bone as before. It disappeared into nothing. Then I noticed that the drop one inch from the bones was beginning to disappear. It was soon gone and in its place, a small blue spot the same hue as the bones.

I flipped a switch on the table that locked the door and brought down the cover meant to keep anything dangerous inside the glass. At the far end of the lab, I threw my gloves into the mini-incinerator, as well as my other PPE, and then just to be extra safe, my clothes. I went through the emergency shower of cold water, and then I put on a set of scrubs. I didn't need to wear PPE with the bones tucked away in the protective glass. The system inside the glass had everything I'd need to look at the evidence, from microscope viewing, to MRI scans, to a robot arm. But a shiver went through me at the thought of the blood disappearing, and I put a layer of protective clothes on anyway.

.　.　.

Sealed Tight

I was on my computer when T.A. walked in, looking perplexed, his hand covering his nose.

"Are you okay?" I asked.

He nodded. As he grabbed up some tissues, he replied, "I'm okay, Sheriff Mora. Billy kicked me out of the van."

"What happened exactly?" I asked.

"My blood landed on the table and then it disappeared. Then she kicked me out."

"Disappeared?" I laughed, but he looked very serious. "Okay. Disappeared." Like we needed anything else weird to happen.

My phone dinged. It was a text message from an unknown number.

This is Billy. Put all the evidence of human and dog remains in a sealed room. You must wear anti-contaminate protection gear. If T.A. helps you, just make sure he's completely suited up. No blood must come anywhere near that evidence!!"

I stood up and wondered what had her so worried and why had T.A.'s blood disappeared.

"Billy wants us suited up. And I need a sealed room?" I shook my head. It wasn't like we had one of those around the station. I pulled open the bottom drawer where I hid the latest in hazmat suits and tossed a bag over to T.A.

I couldn't think of one place that might be safe. Then Lane Anderson's truck drove by.

I grabbed my phone and called his office.

"Asbestos Abatement, this is Kathy."

"Kathy! This is Sheriff Mora. I have an emergency at the office. Can I have Lane's cell phone number?"

Ten minutes later, Lane and his two coworkers were sealing up one of the jail cells.

"What made you think of this?" T.A. asked as we watched them cover the room in sheets of plastic.

"I had to have asbestos removed from my house a few years ago. The company had to seal off a space completely to make it safe for asbestos abatement. They make it airtight to keep any asbestos from escaping."

He nodded. "Smart move."

As soon as they were done, T.A. and I donned our hazmat suits and walked over to the tables with the remains. Only now did I let my mind wonder what Billy had found. What could make blood disappear?

Luckily, the boxes were few and light. There were three for each of the dogs and two for each of the other human victims. We placed them in the middle of the cell, surrounded by red plastic. It was like being in one of those disaster movies — dark colors, looking at everything through a clear mask from inside the suit. After the last box, I closed the door behind me and used the tape Lane had given me to seal off the door.

I went back to where we had stored the boxes and sprayed the area with bleach. Then Lane put us through the decontamination shower and put the suits into a biohazard bag.

Still, my skin crawled when I was back in my uniform.

I was paying Lane when one of his workers set the newspaper on my desk. "This came while you were busy."

I could see the headline from where I stood. *Mysterious Deaths Leave Only Bones.*

"Thanks." Reluctantly, I picked up the newspaper. The article was pretty good, Darren mentioned that the town sheriff works very hard, has a black belt, and has her hands full. Too true.

But, at the end of the article, "photos were redacted by the sheriff because there are some details she doesn't want the public to know."

"Damn it, Darren."

I shoved the newspaper away. Still no word from Billy. I glanced out at the truck and hoped she was okay.

* * *

T.A. had asked to read through the files from the incidents, so he was sitting at my computer chewing on the end of a pencil while he scrolled through the documents.

A breath of fresh air was what I needed. As I walked down Main Street, Erica, the town psychic, came running out of her storefront. Her flowy robe and long black hair flew behind her, and her purple beads jostled.

"Sheriff! A ghost has put a curse on this town."

"A ghost?" I asked, curious where Erica was going to take this idea.

Erica played with a strand of her beads and nodded. "There's a deep malevolence hovering over the town. A swirl of anger and hatred. And..." She closed her eyes and lifted her hands into the air. "And it smells of alcohol wipes?" She seemed surprised at her last statement and opened her eyes.

"Wipes?" I asked.

She nodded.

Darren must have told her about the smell at Jackie's house, even though I had asked him not to share it. It wasn't in the newspaper article, at least. "Erica, if we determine that the problem is a ghost, you'll be the first person I come to."

She nodded, satisfied with that answer, and flowed back to her store. Although not a believer, I had always loved her place. The front window was filled with colorful tarot card packages, candles, stones, a few doll house-size pyramids, and hanging all-seeing-eye designs.

In the plaza, the trees were dropping leaves like mad

now. The ground was a carpet of yellow, peach, and orange. The street lights were coming on as I waived at Father Tom across the street. He waived back. I picked up three to-go plates and coffees from the diner. Larry, the owner, turned off the neon open sign as I walked out the door, a prelude to what should be a quiet town evening.

The door to the mobile lab opened as I walked by, and Billy stepped out dressed in blue scrubs. I felt like I had been holding my breath this whole time.

"Billy! I'm glad to see you."

Billy nodded. "And I'm glad to see you."

She nabbed a coffee off the tray and drank it while we walked into the station.

We didn't say anything until everyone was eating at a card table I had set up as far from the storage room as possible, but I could feel it in the air — Billy had something she wanted to tell us.

Little Killers

After a couple of bites of meatloaf, Billy started, "A terrible conversation for dinner, but our culprits are tiny blood-sucking bugs."

I shivered and brushed off my arms. "Bugs?"

"If it hadn't been for your intern, I might never have found them. They were dormant once they lost access to liquids, but that tiny drop of blood woke them up long enough to drink it."

T.A.'s eyes grew wide, but he continued digging into his meatloaf.

I tried not to think of the fact that I had picked up every one of those bones. Of course, with gloves and other protections on, but the idea that I might have died if I had touched them without protection made me shiver again.

Billy continued, "The bugs are also slightly radioactive. I've pretty much traced them to Japanese tatami bugs. Those are Japanese bed bugs that live on human blood. I think someone has genetically modified them to be smaller and deadlier."

"How small are we talking?" I asked.

"Think dust mite size, you can't see them with the naked eye."

Billy pulled a picture out of her pocket and set it on the table. Both T.A. and I leaned in to see it better. It was taken from a microscope, the bug had black legs with red lines at the joints and a red backside. I wondered if the red color was from blood.

I pushed the meatloaf away.

T.A. and Billy seemed less affected, they continued to eat with gusto.

At least I could sip at my coffee without feeling queasy.

Billy pointed at the picture. "Luckily, they don't

have wings, otherwise they could devastate this small town in no time."

I shuddered. "Are you sure it's not just some natural evolution or something?"

Billy nodded. "Absolutely. These things originated from Japanese tatami bugs, the radiation proves that. If these things had traveled from Japan to here naturally, we would have seen a lot more dead bodies."

I wrapped my head around what she was saying. "So, someone has modified these bugs and is using them on individuals."

"Yes," she answered.

I leaned forward. "We have a murderer." This news was somewhat comforting. No ghost, no unknown, this was a person, and that meant we could find them. But, the use of the bugs worried me. "This someone could release these bugs anywhere, even in public."

Billy nodded.

T.A. shook his head. "Those dogs that died. The murderer tied them up. You mentioned in your report that you found a collar around their neck bones, and they were tied down to a metal ring."

I nodded.

He continued, "And the people that died were all in a secluded place. I think the murderer was using the dogs as part of an experiment. Then he moved on to target people, people he hated, I bet."

I was thinking the same thing but was interested in

how he had come to that idea. "And why do you think that?"

"Crime analysis 101. Criminals often escalate to more serious offenses. It's like when someone starts a new job, they learn how to do things with more skill."

"I agree. And, knowing that an actual person behind this is ...." I wasn't quite sure of the right word.

"Actionable." Billy chimed in. "I say we take a more careful look at the dog owners and find the connection between everyone."

But I still had questions. "Wait, are they eating the skin too, and what about the blue color left behind?"

Billy took her last big bite of food and leaned back. "I have to send a sample to the CDC. I don't have the knowledge or experience to dive into this deeper."

I pulled a whiteboard over to the table and wrote the names of the dogs, dog owners, and the three human victims. I had seen TV shows where the detectives put up perfect pictures of every victim as if the police departments had access to some magical database of people getting professional photos right before they died. I did not have access to that database. Names would have to do.

"I think I should start by interviewing the dog owners."

Billy nodded. "Agree. We should start by interviewing the dog owners."

I was relieved she was willing to help with the legwork.

"I'll interview the owners of Baskin," I said.

Billy grabbed a file off the top of the pile. "I'm taking Prince Silver Streak, the show dog, and his owners. He was the first, I think that might make him special in some way. T.A., that leaves you Rainbow."

She handed T.A. the file.

I wasn't sure about having T.A. interview anyone, but Billy was on it. "T.A. what kind of questions are you going to ask the owners?"

T.A. looked off in the distance and used his fingers to count off his questions. "Ask them about neighbors or anyone that didn't like them or their dog. Find out their background, like where they work or go to the gym. Plus, any other questions that might lead to other questions or ideas."

Billy looked at me when she said, "I think that's good."

I nodded at them both, but then I realized how late it was. The sun had gone down hours ago and we wouldn't continue to be productive if we didn't take care of ourselves as well.

"How about we start our interviews first thing in the morning?" I suggested.

T.A. nodded.

Billy stood up, "I'm going to get a sample for the

CDC ready for tomorrow. I've requested they send someone to pick it up."

As I locked up the office, I wondered what sort of person would use bugs. The perp had probably gotten into the homes and placed the bugs on their victims, but had they watched them die? Had Jackie suffered? She had been facing the phone, trying to get help probably. It made my blood boil to think about what someone had done to her.

Dark Figure

I sat on my back porch, a glass of red wine in my hand, and listened to the crickets and frogs. Steve lay on my lap, softly snoring, and keeping me warm like a little furnace.

The trees along the back of my property creaked in the wind, and beyond that was the park. With the porch light off, I could see the stars. I never had this kind of view in the city.

Then the chorus of the night changed — there was a whole section of frogs and crickets that stopped. That generally meant there was an animal in the woods disturbing the night crawlers. I leaned forward, straining my eyes to see if a deer was moving through the yard.

I closed my eyes for a moment to get them used to the dark. When I opened them, I gasped. There was an outline of a person standing in front of a big tree smack in the middle of the tree line. The tree stood silvery in the starlight, and someone was standing in front of it. The outline was masculine.

I had no idea how long he had been there. Had he seen me turn off the porch light and knew I was sitting outside? Was he armed? I wanted to flip this situation and put him on the defensive, but I didn't have a lot of options.

If I moved to turn on the porch light, he'd probably run before I could see him.

"Who's out there?" I yelled, expecting him to react.

If he ran to my right, he would be taking the trail to the park. If he ran left, I might be able to cut him off by running around the house to the side yard where that trail came out.

The hairs on my neck stood up as the figure didn't move. He knew I could see him, certainly. Then he slowly turned and walked into the darkness of the trees to my right.

As soon as he was out of sight I picked up Steve who snorted at being woken. I locked the back door, locked the dog door, set Steve on his dog bed, and then dashed out to my car. I drove through my neighborhood as fast as I could around to the Pond View parking lot where the trail ended, but I was too late. There were no cars in the lot, but one car was driving up the hill next to the park. It could have been my lurker, but there was no way to know for sure.

I followed the car for half an hour, and it was still driving on a road that led out of town, so I turned around and headed back home.

The First Victims

As I drove to my friend's place, the former owners of Baskin, I wondered if I'd ask the right questions. Would my interview be as good as Billy's? She was trained by the FBI, after all. Then I shook my head. I wasn't some greenhorn, and this wasn't the first murder I'd had to solve, and, unfortunately, even in this small town, it probably wouldn't be the last.

The Ludlows lived in a ranch-style brick house, one that had been built probably fifty years ago. The landscaping had recently been updated. The Japanese maple was beginning to show its fall colors, and the grass was clipped short.

I could see the side yard gate. No lock, but then why would anyone have to lock up their dog, that is up until now.

Sarah Ludlow answered the door in her slippers and pink flowered robe. I double-checked my watch — 9:30 AM. "Hello, Sarah, I'm here to talk to you more about Baskin."

Sarah nodded. "Come on in, Mora."

She led me into the living room where Ray was watching the news in his lounge chair, a cat purring on his lap. I couldn't imagine that these two could have ever upset anyone, let alone someone who could genetically manipulate bugs.

Ray turned off the television, and Sarah motioned to the couch. Sarah started, "Last time you were here, you asked me if any of the neighbors had gotten mad about Baskin. My answer hasn't changed. He never barked or caused problems. He was the sweetest dog I'd ever had."

"Thanks for thinking more about it. I want to dig a little deeper. Do you get out of the house much?"

Sarah nodded. "I work part-time at the university in Accounts Payable for the Research Department."

"Wow. That's more than an hour's drive from here. Seems a long way to go."

Sarah shrugged. "It's good pay for a retired school-teacher, and I don't mind the drive."

"Anyone there give you a hard time?"

Sarah laughed. "There are a lot of strong personalities at the university. The director goes off on crazy tangents, and most of the researchers feel like if you aren't the solution, you're holding their research back."

"Anyone at the top of that list?"

"Ah." She sat back and looked up. "It's just impossible to pick one person."

Ray leaned forward in his chair. "What about that researcher that gave you the creeps?"

Sarah shook her head. "That was a couple of months ago. I don't even know his name."

"What happened?" I prompted.

"I was walking through the hallway. It was late, and I had been finishing up the end-of-month accounts. This researcher came running through the halls, and apparently, I wasn't moving fast enough. He said something to me and gave me the weirdest look while he brushed past me."

Ray interjected, "He said, 'Don't you have better things to do than to slow down progress?'"

"You remember that?" Sarah shook her head.

Ray nodded. "When you told me about the incident, it struck me how peevish this guy was."

"But you didn't know his name?" I asked.

"No."

"Did he know yours?"

Sarah looked up again. "Maybe? When the admin staff need help, I'll go and set up for meetings, or whatever they need, so he's probably seen me around. My desk in the research office is next to the main desk, so he could have often seen me there. I don't pay much attention to who comes and goes from the office."

"But he gave you the creeps?"

She nodded. "It wasn't just that look or what he said. There was plenty of room in the hallway for him to get by. It was like he was looking for a fight."

"What did he look like?"

"He has salt-and-pepper hair and ice-blue eyes. He's also a little taller than me. Five-foot-six, maybe?"

My heart was pounding as I wrapped up the interview but made sure Sarah would call me if she remembered anything else.

Ice-blue eyes. One week ago, Jackie and I had a glass of wine at her place, and she told me about the man with the ice-blue eyes that had come on to her at the local dry cleaners. She had rebuffed him. "He wasn't bad looking. Graying hair and a little taller than me. But when he looked at me with those ice-blue eyes, it creeped me out. He said that I'd regret that decision. Like that's ever going to happen." She had laughed.

She hadn't described him any more than that, and I hadn't asked.

But a lot of men had blue eyes. It didn't mean this was the guy, but my gut was saying this was the guy.

I arrived at the station and kept my cool, I wasn't ready to share my gut feeling. T.A. and Billy were comparing notes.

"Ah," Billy said as she saw me enter. "We just started sharing our interviews."

I sat heavily in my office chair and swiveled around to face them. "Anything connecting with you two?"

Billy pointed at the whiteboard. Next to the dog names they had written *neighbors?, coworkers?, and university?*

"Not yet," T.A. answered.

"Why did someone write university?"

Billy responded. "Miss Humboldt who owns Prince Silver Streak works at the university."

I walked to the board and circled both Sarah's and Miss Humboldt's names. "T.A., if I remember correctly, Leana Lewis is the main owner of Rainbow? Her husband wasn't around when I first went to see them."

T.A. nodded. "She said she's getting a divorce. He's been out of the house for a couple of months now."

I crossed out Richard Lewis and circled Leana's name. Then I circled the two women who were killed.

Billy nodded, "That's exactly what I was thinking. He is mainly targeting women."

"And why do you say 'he'?" I asked.

"Truthfully, I don't know. There are profilers who could look at the case and give us more information. It just feels right to put 'he' on this."

T.A. stood up and spoke as if he was a teacher. "There are several factors that point to a male suspect, like the fact that he didn't just kill them. He choose a gruesome way for these people to die. The way a person is murdered often tells us the gender of the murderer."

Billy saluted him with her coffee. "Thanks, Professor Parks. And, as per Mora's report, the finger bones of Jackie were found with her phone. That leads me to think that she was alive and aware of what was happening. Absolutely gruesome. But these murders also point to the type of man. These are thought out, and carefully constructed. He researched his victims, probably watched them, and figured out their schedules."

I inhaled deeply while I thought of that man hiding in the shadows the other night.

"What?" Billy asked.

I shook my head. "It's probably nothing, but there was a man at the edge of my property last night. I didn't get a look at him. When I yelled at him, he took his time leaving."

Billy let out a long breath and then nodded towards the whiteboard. "Our suspect obviously has issues with women. He would resist being scared away by you. This could be him."

"But I haven't interviewed any suspects. Why come after me?"

T.A. grabbed the newspaper from my desk. "Anything in this?" He started to read it, and I realized, yes there was.

He read out loud, "Nothing in this town happens without the sheriff figuring it out. She's solved every murder that's ever happened on her watch, and she sure won't stop now."

T.A. held up the page with my picture on it. "Looks great."

Billy chimed in, "If he thinks you can catch him, he might consider that an affront to his careful plans."

I shook my head. "Great. No more wine on the back porch for a while. I can get some more cameras to put in the backyard. There's no way he can get inside, I have cameras that alert me if anything moves."

Billy looked off into the distance. "If he's decided you're his next target, we need to be really careful. He could leave those bugs on your car seat or anywhere else you find yourself alone — your front door handle, or even leave them in the backyard to get that sweet dog of yours." She was pointing at my pic of Steve on my desk.

My heart sank at the idea of sweet Steve being a target.

T.A. may have sensed my concern. "But don't freak out or anything. We don't know any of this for sure."

It did feel as if it could be the case. "But if it is right, maybe we can set a trap. I could go home as usual, and leave the curtains in the back open. Have a stakeout in my backyard to try and catch whoever this is?"

"We'll need a few more people."

T.A. picked up his phone. "I know some guys."

A Trap Set

I had been hanging around my kitchen for hours and nothing had happened. As I stood in my kitchen, I felt like a fraud. Had I imagined the man in the woods?

"Still no sign of anyone." A masculine voice whispered into the coms. I thought it was Kevin, one of T.A.'s college friends who'd come to join us, all of whom were hiding in the woods.

Every minute that passed I felt like an idiot. "Maybe you should all just go home?" I said into the walkie.

Billy spoke up, "Hey, if all perps showed up on the first night of a stakeout, police work would be way easier than it is. Even if this turns out to be nothing, I feel better knowing that we've kept an eye out for you."

It took a couple of hours for Billy to call it a night for everyone. "Mora, make sure everything is locked up tight. We'll try this again tomorrow night."

I had already dropped Steve off at a friend's place for safety, so the house was terribly quiet after everyone left.

* * *

Once again, we all met at the office at the same early hour. All of us had coffee in hand when my phone rang.

The voice on the other end was frantic and shaky. "Sheriff! This is Mrs. Skibitski. I clean Professor Sanderson's house."

"Yes, Mrs. Skibitski."

"He's ... well, I found a pile of bones in the foyer, and I'm worried it's him."

I sighed. "Stay away from the bones, Mrs. Skibitski. I'll be there as quickly as I can. What's the address?"

As I wrote it down, T.A. grabbed some fresh hazard suits.

Billy grabbed her jacket. "We're coming with you. Where are we going?"

"Out to one of the big houses. It's going to be a long drive."

Inside the foyer we found Mrs. Skibitski sitting on the edge of a chair and five feet away were the bones. Before putting on my mask, I made a note of the scents in the air that had been the same at all the other crime scenes — rubbing alcohol, cologne, and dry death.

Billy checked on Mrs. Skibitski. "Mrs. Skibitski, you didn't go near the bones, did you?"

The housekeeper shook her head. "Dear me, no. This is as close as I was willing to go. I just don't understand," Mrs. Skibitski continued. "I was here yesterday to cook him his dinner and everything was normal. How could this happen?"

Neither of us said anything. How do you tell a nice old lady that her boss was eaten by blood-sucking bugs?

Billy helped her up and escorted her outside.

Per his instructions, T.A. stayed near me.

I knelt near the bones and took copious photos. It was uncanny. One of the professor's arms was stretched out towards the door and the other bent with the hand near his head, like he had been crawling towards the door when he was demolished by the bugs.

I wondered where he had been when it started. His path could be littered with dormant bugs just waiting for someone to set them back to eating blood and flesh.

The carpet didn't look much different at first, but then I could see it — drag marks where he had pulled himself along. There were bits of blue and skin along the trail. I set cones along his path and followed the marks to a chair in the living room.

I went to the front door. "Mrs. Skibitski, did he always spend time in his lounger in the living room?"

She nodded. "Every night. He likes, I mean, he liked to watch those DIY shows about fixing up houses. Not sure why, never did a thing to this house."

That explained why the killer hadn't shown up at my place. He'd been busy here. That nugget of information made me realize I should listen to my gut. Even though there could be a million reasons why someone had been outside my house the other night, it made sense to me that it was ice-blue eyes.

"And you call the deceased a professor. Did he work at the university?"

"Oh, yes. Very proud of that. He taught medical students and was working on some research, as well. He was excited to get published. I guess it's a big thing for researchers."

"What was he researching?"

She shook her head. "No idea. He went on and on

about one thing or another. I didn't understand a word of it."

T.A. came around the corner. "Billy, there's a purple container sitting in the kitchen. It's like the one Sheriff Mora took a photo of at the last scene."

Billy acknowledged him with a nod.

I felt a twinge of pride for catching the purple container at Jackie's. This would at least be another clue to connect to the killer.

We were finally done collecting evidence by 2 PM.

We sealed up the house and headed back to the office. As I moved the evidence into the isolation room, I hoped that this would be the last time I'd have to do this.

I joined T.A. and Billy in the office. We all sagged in our chairs, tired and a bit deflated.

"T.A., can you order us some lunch to be delivered?"

He nodded and then hovered over his phone, presumably doing some food research.

I took a deep breath, a little nervous to share my thoughts with Billy. "I know we're all exhausted, but I think our guy is a man with ice-blue eyes and salt-and-pepper hair who works at the university. I want to track him down."

Billy shook her head. "But we still haven't interviewed the friends and family of the people who were killed."

I tried to put my gut feeling into words. "Jackie told me about a guy she had a run-in with that sounded similar to the guy Sarah Ludlow, Baskin's owner, had a problem with at the university. I think it's him. The university should be able to help me track him down."

Billy stretched up, reaching to the ceiling. "That seems like a long shot. I'd rather work on the absolutes, like having another stake out at your place for that man who was hiding in the woods. And, in the meantime, examine the purple containers from the last two scenes. I want to see if there's anything there for evidence. Besides, it will be 3 PM before we get lunch, then we eat, and then it's an hour to reach the university. I don't think it's going to be helpful to go to the university tonight."

I sighed. She was right. By 4:30 there would be a stream of cars heading out of the college campus and we'd be lucky to find anyone still at their desk. But I was still certain about my hunch.

I picked up the phone, but all my calls to the university research offices went to voicemail. After okaying T.A.'s food order, I leaned back in my chair and noticed that crumpled note in the trash.

It was Darren's list of experts. I pulled it out of the trash and flattened the note down. These experts more than likely worked at the university, and they might know this mysterious blue-eyed researcher. The housing development was thirty minutes away. I could find the addresses while I waited for food, then head out and see if anyone was home to interview.

On my list from Darren was Jeremy Horton, Elizabeth Crane-Reed, Michael Green, and David Sheahan. I crossed off Elizabeth's name and found the addresses of the others. By the time I finished my meal, I had a list to start with.

I texted Billy that I'd see her at my place for the stakeout.

"T.A., I'm heading out. I'll see you and your friends at my place after dark."

T.A. followed me outside. "Are you going to try and track down that guy?"

I took a deep breath and nodded. "Yes. I can't just sit here and wait for the evening and hope the killer shows up at my place."

"Can I come with you? I want to see an expert at work."

I smiled. "Way to get yourself a ride. We're going to check out a list of experts my newspaper friend gave me."

I wasn't expecting to find my icy blue-eyed murderer on this list, but Jeremy Horton answered the door. He was the right height and his hair was more salt than pepper. And those eyes, blue but maybe not so icy blue.

"Mr. Horton?"

"Doctor Horton, yes."

"Doctor, I'm Sheriff Gentry, and this is my intern T.A. I was hoping to ask you some questions about someone you might know."

"Sure, come on in."

I kept my distance from him as we walked in and T.A. shut the door behind us. However, one look at his house told me this wasn't the guy. He led us into a study in a state of what I considered to be the natural order of things. Books were piled in haphazard ways, pieces of paper and stickie notes were everywhere. In the middle of it all, a copper bust of a woman's face. I walked over to read the inscription.

"Dame Mary Lucy Cartwright," I read.

He smiled and nodded. "Yes, not only a distant relative but one of the founding women of the chaos theory."

This was not the guy. This house felt comforting, and he thought women were worthy of monuments.

"I'm wondering if you know a researcher from the university. He has salt-and pepper hair, ice-blue eyes, and might be doing research into bug genetics."

"Not genetics," T.A. broke in. "He's involved in manipulating their genes." He glanced at me, "Genetics would be researching their genes but not changing them."

"Oh, okay." I appreciated the distinction.

"Bugs?" Dr. Horton leaned back in his chair. "I

know a few researchers are looking into insects, like roaches and bed bugs."

"Bed bugs?" I asked.

"Roaches?" T.A. asked.

"I don't think any of the insect researchers have published anything yet. Until they do, they're usually very quiet about what they're working on. The insect research only really took off recently."

"As for roaches," Dr. Horton continued. "I heard they're working on putting cameras on them and using remotes to make them change direction."

"Whoa, remote control roaches. That's cool."

I got us back on the important trail. "And bed bugs?"

"A few studies are going on, I don't know much about them."

I thought about how I could find out. "Do you think there's someone I could call at the university who could tell me?"

He shook his head. "The university protects its secrets. I would assume you'd need to go in with a warrant."

I nodded. "Thank you, Dr. Horton."

Our next stop was Michael Green. He answered the door with his golf bag over his shoulder. The covers on his clubs almost matched the red of his hair.

He stepped outside. "I was just heading to the golf course. Can I help you?"

"Dr. Green, I'm Sheriff Gentry, and this is my

intern, T.A. I was hoping to ask you some questions about someone you might know — salt-and-pepper hair and ice-blue eyes who works at the university."

As he walked to his car he responded, "Yes, sounds like a couple of guys I know. But, when you say ice-blue, that makes me think of Dr. Sheahan."

"Dr. David Sheahan?" I asked, recalling the next name on my list.

Dr. Green nodded.

"Do you know what he researches?"

"I think it has something to do with forensic anthropology. We don't talk very much." He paused before getting into his car. "But if you interview him, well, maybe have your intern do the interview. I've heard he tends to get confrontational with women."

As he drove away, I felt a bit uncertain. How could forensic anthropology have anything to do with bugs? Was I off the mark chasing blue eyes? Was he just a jerk with women but not the bug man we were looking for?

I was ringing the bell at Dr. Sheahan's house when my phone buzzed.

It was Billy. "Mora, it's time to set up at your house for our perp."

"Okay. Be there soon." But I waited in case someone answered the door, but there wasn't a peep from inside. I guessed it was too much to ask for everyone to be home.

* * *

I cleaned the kitchen for the fifteenth time and glanced out the back window into the darkness. Nothing.

Billy had said he was more than likely methodical and patient, and that nothing might happen tonight. But my gut was telling me he was stepping up his murders.

My doorbell rang, the usual sound making me grasp my chest in surprise.

A glance at my doorbell camera displayed a deliveryman and I was expecting some dog bones. I said into the coms, "Someone's at the door. I'm going to go answer it."

Voices came all at once on the coms.

"I want someone at the front asap."

"I'm on it."

"Sheriff, don't answer it yet."

I walked to the door and could spy through the front window a white unmarked van, one of those that commonly delivered packages. I opened the door and there was a package sitting on my porch, the delivery man was walking away.

The package was too small for my order and something in the way he walked inspired me to chase after him. "Hey! I don't remember ordering anything. Are you sure you have the right house?"

He turned and in the light of the street lamp, I could

see his ice-blue eyes. "I don't make mistakes." The hat hid most of his salt-and-pepper hair.

My blood froze. I was hit with a hint of cologne that I had smelled at all the murder locations, along with an astringent scent like hand wipes.

"David Sheahan, I need you to stay right here."

His eyes narrowed at the name. He pulled a gun out of his pocket. "Actually, I need you to open that package. Move along, Mora."

Where was my help? They would have had to go around the neighborhood to get to the front, and either direction would take them a few minutes. I walked slowly to the front porch.

"Move faster." He kicked me in the back, and I grabbed his leg, pulling it forward as I turned. The gun was pointed in the air, and he lost his balance. His face contorted in rage as he fell to the ground.

I stomped on his hand holding the gun as he pulled the trigger. The bullet hit the ground, sending up dirt and rocks a few feet from us.

Then he punched my knee and forced me to jump back. He pointed the gun at me, and I was sure I was dead.

Instead, he ran his finger through his hair with his free hand as he stood, then stepped backward to the box. He picked it up and held it out toward me. "Open it."

I knew what was in that box. I wasn't going to die that way.

A shot rang out. My friends were close.

David Sheahan fell back onto the grass, a stain of blood reaching across the fabric of his shirt, then the blood began to disappear.

He dropped his gun and used his hands to wipe at his chest. "No! No!"

The box had a bullet hole in it too. I needed to put some distance between us and stepped back. Unfortunately, the movement brought his attention back to me.

He rolled onto his chest and struggled onto his feet. "Give me a hug, bitch." He lunged forward.

I took my only option. I punched him hard in the face. He staggered back, and then there was another gunshot. David Sheahan reached for his shoulder where the new bullet wound was spreading blood. He stumbled back onto the rocks in my yard.

Billy was standing next to me, out of breath, gun ready to shoot again. She reached out to touch my shoulder, but I leapt away. "Don't touch me. I don't know if I have any of those bugs on me. Don't touch him either."

The perp smiled, "Oh, you'll die just like this." The blood on his shoulder was disappearing. Then his chest began to collapse from the middle out. He closed his eyes and within minutes there was nothing but bones.

I looked at my hands, trying to see if I could find any sign, tears coming to my eyes. T.A. and his friends came running and stopped short when I motioned them to stay back. "I don't know if I'm about to die a horrible death, so stay back."

I kept my eyes on my hands, hoping that I could live another day.

Billy took a pair of glasses out of her pocket. "I'm going to get close enough to look."

I stretched out my hands and turned them over so she could see both sides with the magnifying glasses.

"I don't see any. I think you got lucky."

I held back the tears. "Just, don't touch me for a little while, to be sure."

* * *

I climbed out of my car and looked up at the monstrosity of a house. It was going to be my pleasure to help tear this place apart to find anything and everything we could about Dr. David Sheahan. Although his ice-blue eyes were gone now, we had dug up a lot of information about him already.

"Sheriff Gentry." The CDC director pointed to the tent they had set up outside the doctor's house. "You can suit up in there. We're about ready to go in."

I nodded, grateful that, with Billy's insistence, we both would be able to go in on the final piece of the murder puzzle. Meanwhile, the CDC was combing over all the old locations of deaths, making sure there were no bugs left. They had found that rubbing alcohol was enough to kill them and keep them from coming back.

Now every person in town was scouring their homes and cars with the stuff to make sure they'd be safe. The town stores would be out of rubbing alcohol for a while now.

The doctor's student intern had spilled a lot of useful information. "He started as a forensic anthropologist and was the whole reason I became his intern. But he hated the mess of flesh on bones and wanted to develop a way to strip dead bodies of flesh quickly without using the current techniques that are very slow. That sent him in a whole new direction of work. He started working with insects to genetically modify them. He did some groundbreaking work on the tiniest of insects."

"The only problem was, the insects he developed only wanted living tissue, they wouldn't remove dead tissue. When his plan didn't pan out, he dropped into a sort of depression. He was angry all the time."

"So, he developed these killer insects, wasn't anyone keeping track of them?"

His student intern sighed. "I talked to management. The university saw no monetary use for them and didn't classify them as a weapon."

"They didn't consider those things a weapon?" I asked.

He nodded.

Billy and I would work to bring the university under charges. Meanwhile, we were ready to find the bugs and destroy them.

Billy, T.A., and I suited up and made our way into the house. The CDC team was just ahead of us, spraying alcohol on the walls, and on every surface.

In the foyer was a glass table with a glass bowl and a shining mirror hanging above. The first room, a study, was more glass, and everything at perfect right angles. The next room was the jackpot — a stack of purple containers, which we were told by the intern were from the university, ordered by mistake by an admin and charged to Dr. Sheahan's research account.

There was no written list of his intended targets, no pictures hanging on the wall of those he felt had wronged him. I assumed we'd eventually find that information in his computer in typed-up notes.

And there, in the corner, a sealed glass case with a magnifying glass. A CDC member sprayed the outside of the container before approaching the magnifying glass. "Shit. This is where he stored them. There are thousands of them in here lying dormant."

I backed out of the room while the team prepared to spray the inside of the case.

Billy and I looked through the rest of the house for clues, but, the rest of the house was much like the foyer and much like Dr. David Sheahan. Cold and empty.

Did you enjoy this story? Please leave a review for the anthology! Reviews sell books.

Sonja Dewing is an award-winning author and publisher. She tends to write thriller/fantasy and always writes strong women. She's an avid hiker, plays roller derby with Elevated Roller Derby, and is taken on walks by her giant puppy Bo. Want more stories? Sign up for her email list and you'll receive one award-winning adventure, *The Glass Mountain*, and one exclusive story to her email list, *The Journal of Benedict Cecil Spafford*. Both stories are prequels to her award-winning fantasy adventure series, *The Idol Makers*. Sign up here: http://eepurl.com/cAzV5v

Misdirection
Pat McGregor

agnolia Mbele found her quarry outside a curtained ER cubicle. Charlene Kowalski was pacing restlessly in the hall, and it took Magnolia three tries to attract her attention. "Ma'am, I am the investigator from the California Department of Public Health. Can we talk?"

Charlene's waist-length hair curtained around her as she spun to face Magnolia, her blue eyes deep pools in her strained face.

"Y-yes," the woman stuttered and looked around for a chair. Magnolia led her to a small cubicle down the hall, and they both sat on the grey furniture.

"I am from the health department," Magnolia started again, "and I am here to investigate your husband's case. The doctors think this is food poisoning rather than flu, and our department looks into all such cases."

Charlene nodded and rubbed her temples. "What do you want to know?"

Magnolia quickly ran Charlene through the basics of the case, reviewing the information the doctor in charge of Sean Kowalski's case had given her. Sean had been vomiting for six hours, and what they'd given him to calm the stomach was working, and he was now resting. The health department had been called in when the labs turned up amatoxins in his bloodstream. These compounds indicated that he'd eaten—or been fed—the deadly *Amanita* mushroom.

Magnolia didn't know why the doctor had ordered the test for toxins, and she would find out before the doctor clocked off shift.

The staff had pumped Sean's stomach and given him activated charcoal. Magnolia was interested in the liver function tests the doctor had ordered. Sean's case was progressing quickly—usually, a patient had twelve to thirty-six hours before liver damage began, but the doctor had been on the ball once the amatoxins were found and had taken the necessary proactive steps.

Dr. Tompkins, the Folsom Mercy Hospital resident overseeing Sean's case, poked his prematurely balding head into the cubicle and smiled at Magnolia and Charlene.

"Good, I've found you. We're admitting Sean and

moving him to a room upstairs. I've ordered a recliner moved in," he nodded at Charlene, "so you can rest. He should sleep for several hours. The liver function tests are inconclusive, so we'll have to rerun them in six hours." He yawned hugely. "Sorry. The next step will be dialysis to remove the toxins from the bloodstream. Do you have any questions?"

Magnolia had several but didn't want to ask them in front of Charlene. "Where can I find you later, Doctor?"

"I'll be around, or in the resident's bunk." He waved his arm to indicate the ER. "It's a moderately busy night, and I'm on duty for another twelve hours." He left as abruptly as he'd arrived.

Magnolia urged Charlene to her feet and suggested they go to the hospital's cafeteria while Sean was being moved. Some food might help the troubled woman, and this would keep her out of the way while the nurses did their work. *I could use another cup of coffee*, Magnolia thought to herself, remembering the small café here had decent coffee even in the middle of the night.

When they had settled down with coffee and sandwiches, Magnolia spoke again. "My job is to find the source of the mushrooms and see how you came in contact with them."

"Mushrooms?" Charlene made a *yuck* face. "Sean hates mushrooms; he would never eat them willingly. We don't forage for mushrooms and haven't had anything with mushrooms in it, I'm sure."

"Walk me through what you did eat yesterday," Magnolia suggested.

Sean and Charlene had left their house at about 7 a.m. to drive up Route 50 to South Lake Tahoe. They'd driven around the massive lake to see the last snow in the Sierras and had eaten at a diner about 1 p.m. They'd gotten home about 6 p.m., and Sean had been feeling funny the last hour or so of the drive. He'd barely made it inside the house before the sickness began, and she'd dragged him to the ER at 10 p.m.

"What diner did you eat at?" Magnolia was taking notes on her little tablet.

"Uh, someplace north of South Lake Tahoe." Charlene rubbed her temples again. "Oh, wait. I have the receipt here somewhere." She dug into her big tote for her wallet and fanned through the slips of paper inside. "Here." She thrust the receipt at Magnolia.

Magnolia took a picture of it then dropped it into an evidence bag. According to the receipt, they'd eaten at Corman's Drive Inn at 1:30 that afternoon and had ordered two lamb stews, a garden salad, coffee, and iced tea—no dessert.

"There were no mushrooms in the stew and none in the salad?"

"I ate the salad too, and I'm not sick. My stew had no mushrooms, but I didn't examine Sean's too closely. They came out of the same pot in the kitchen, I'm pretty sure because we could see into the kitchen and watch them prepare our food."

Magnolia checked her watch. She'd have time to go home and sleep, then drive to Tahoe in the morning. She'd call in an evidence team to investigate the diner.

"This is the only place you ate?"

"Yes, we ate sandwiches we brought with us. We wanted to spend time out in the sunshine, not stuck in a restaurant."

"I'll need those sandwiches, anything you have left over," Magnolia cautioned the woman.

"They're in the cooler in the car," Charlene replied. "Sean was so sick I never unpacked after the trip."

While Charlene went to get the cooler, Magnolia sent her team instructions. The texts would wake the team, but she couldn't help that. Corman's was a 24-hour diner; they needed to get there and get samples as soon as possible. There could be other victims—accidental or on purpose.

There were still so many questions to answer at this phase of the investigation, and Magnolia wished for her bed. She'd been up late doing paperwork the night before and had hoped to catch up on sleep tonight. *So much for that*, she thought as she drank her coffee.

Looking at her tablet, Magnolia could see her reflection in the flat light of the café. Her eyes looked tired. She had her father's hazel eyes, startlingly pale beside her mother's dark espresso skin. Her sibs all had dark eyes; only she had the light-colored eyes of her Scandi-navian father.

But those eyes had bags under them tonight. She would have to get some sleep soon. She ran her fingers through her hair and scrubbed at her scalp, mussing her short dark hair. She would get Charlene settled, then go home and see if she could get four or five hours of sleep.

2.

The sous chef saw the CDPH investigation team enter the diner with their boxes of equipment, PPE, and checklists. Moving confidently, she rolled up her knives in their sleek leather case, grabbed her flask of special tea from the shelf where she'd stashed it, and slipped out the back door. Finding a job as a sous chef in these small restaurants was easy, so she'd find another and set up again.

Sitting in the chilly cab of her aging F-150 truck, she thought over the last few days. She had known that guy was the right one to dose with her tea. She grinned to herself. He was obnoxious and posturing, and the wife needed release. She had poured a tablespoon of her special brew into his stew, feeling confident it would work. The arrival of the CDPH was her corrob-oration.

The special tea never failed. It was almost time to brew some more. Three pounds of dried amanita mushrooms were in a box in the back seat; she'd find a motel with a kitchenette and make more extract tonight.

Humming to herself, she headed the truck down Highway 50 toward Placerville.

3.

A week later, Magnolia sat in a borrowed cubicle on the hospital's IT floor and stared at pictures of mushrooms. *Amanita phalloides*, to be exact—the death cap mushroom. This little plant was killing Sean Kowalski, and she had no idea how he'd ingested it. None of the foods or utensils tested from Sean's home or the diner had traces, and they'd ruled out Charlene having a motive for murder. Charlene was now in a hospital bed, sedated, having worried herself into a fit after two days without sleep.

Anders Sigismundo, Magnolia's lab crew lead technician, sat beside her, staring at the pictures some professional photographer had taken of the beautiful and deadly mushrooms. Anders popped his gum. "What next, boss?"

"I'm not certain. We don't have any more victims. The only strange thing is that the cook at the diner quit the morning after Sean was poisoned, but she was a drifter, they said. Paid by check. Gone with the wind."

Anders popped his gum reflectively. "We didn't find any mushrooms, either."

"Not a one."

"If the cook did it, how did she do it?"

"Good question."

They sat in contemplation a while longer. Then Magnolia's phone beeped, a two-tone ring that sounded loud in the quiet workspace.

"Holy shit. We've got another one."

"Where?"

"Downstairs. Couple came in from Diamond Springs, same symptoms as Sean, except they kept the stomach contents."

"Why'd they do that?"

"They read the newspaper."

After shutting down her computer and plugging in the anti-theft cable, Magnolia headed for the stairs, Anders right behind her. The metal stairs rang under their pounding feet, and Anders jumped down the last three steps to jar on the landing.

They arrived at the ER cubicle in time to see a nurse labeling a jar of nasty-looking goop and to be introduced to an older couple, Betty and Harris, who looked very green and quite sick. Anders smiled all around and grabbed the sample from the waiting nurse, who looked moderately offended.

Magnolia greeted Dr. Tompkins, who had nabbed the chance to oversee this case. "We already sent the samples Betty brought to the lab as well as some blood tests for amatoxins testing," he crowed. "There are too many similarities with Kowalski."

He filled them in. Betty and Harris had ordered the special of the day, lamb stew, at a diner in Placerville, and by the time they got home, they were spewing from both ends. Betty had read the story in the paper about Sean Kowalski, so they collected their samples and took off to the hospital out of what they hoped was an excess of caution.

Magnolia questioned them further—no, they hadn't seen the cook at the diner, and no, they hadn't ever eaten there before. They had been visiting Gold Bug Park and decided to cap the day off with dinner.

Tompkins was ready to start the activated charcoal routine on the couple, hoping to keep them out of danger since they were starting treatment so many hours earlier than Sean. He already had IVs running and had administered meds to stop the vomiting and diarrhea.

Magnolia perched on a chair in the hallway and tapped her notes into her Teams application, keeping her staff aware of the events. Anders had alerted the evidence team, and they were already on their way to the diner in Placerville to collect their samples and question the personnel.

Anders had shared with Magnolia the lab results on the samples from Betty and Harris—there were no actual amanita mushrooms in the stomach contents, but there was a concentrated extract. Presumably, someone had made amanita mushroom gravy or broth and added it to the lamb stew. As there were only two victims, it looked as though the mushroom extract had been added to their portions only.

Magnolia headed out to her blue Prius. On the drive up the hill to Placerville, she dictated questions to her tablet. They were in no particular order, but to her mind, they were the most urgent issues that needed answers.

Were there any new hires at the diner? Where did they buy their mushrooms? How many servings of the stew had gone out? Had any regulars been sick?

Magnolia arrived at the diner and questioned the manager. The new cook had been on duty when the older couple arrived. No, she wasn't there now, but they had her address. She lived in a cabin in Strawberry, one of the summer rentals. No, she wasn't due in until tomorrow. Yes, they had hired her just a few days ago.

Magnolia called her contact at the sheriff's office to get somebody to check out that address.

4.

The cook stirred a pot over her campfire and laughed heartily. By now, the investigators would have discovered that the cabin in Strawberry was vacant. She'd never lived there. She was camping in the national forest, towing a camper behind her F-150. She was so far ahead of the law. Now, she'd have to resist the urge to use her special tea on anyone for a while. Two days apart had been too close for comfort. But that old bossy couple had been irresistible. They'd been rude to the waitress and talked interminably on their phones while waiting to be served. On speaker, no less. Good riddance.

She remembered her mother teaching her about the tea. Long ago, when they lived in Maine. Mama only used it on genuinely evil people. But these people she was targeting were the evils of the modern world. Privileged assholes, mostly. No one would miss them. Most of the time, people thought the stomach flu got them. And if they didn't die, it was a good lesson.

The fire crackled under her soup pot. The soup was thick and rich, great to eat on these cooler nights up in the foothills. No mushrooms for her, though. Her mama taught her that any mushroom could be turned poison in the hands of Satan, and so she was never to eat any. She never had. She never would.

5.

Magnolia punched the End button on her phone and sighed—only moderately good news. Two weeks in, Betty and Harris were turning the corner—quick action had done the trick, and their liver function tests were returning to normal. They'd probably always have to watch their diets and stay off things like Tylenol, but they would live. Sean was another story—his liver function had never recovered, and now he was being put on a liver transplant list. It was a good thing that he was a non-drinker, or he'd never have made the list. Charlene had started a GoFundMe campaign to cover the cost of the transplant—the couple had crummy health insurance. *The Sacramento Bee* was advertising the fundraising campaign and sponsoring Sean.

Henrietta had flown the coop. She'd been a ghost in Strawberry, never living in the cabin she'd listed as her address, and she didn't have a local bank account. The checks she'd cashed went to one of those online banks, where she did all the banking with her cell phone and debit card. There'd been no activity on the debit card since they started tracking her, and they didn't even know if Henrietta Lackey was her real name. Magnolia had a forensic accountant working on the case, but he'd only found dead ends and disappearing accounts.

The true luck of the case was there were no more victims—at least, no one had reported pernicious stomach flu or death from amatoxins. She was tracking all of Northern California and had contacts in SoCal doing the same, in the hope they'd catch the "Death Cap Killer," as the paper called her, before she struck again. Magnolia had also contacted her opposite numbers in Oregon and Nevada.

Magnolia scrubbed her hands through her hair,

massaging her scalp with her fingers. Other cases were piling up, but she felt Henrietta wasn't done yet. How to track the woman? How to find her before she made someone else ill? How did she choose her victims?

To hell with it, she thought. One night's peace was what she needed, so she'd leave work at the office and go out for pizza and beer. Picking up her phone, she punched call for one of her contacts.

"Mamma? Mags. Hey, I'm craving beer and pizza for dinner. Want to go with me? Yes, tonight. Work's been beastly and I want to relax, and I thought it was high time we visited." She listened, laughed, then shook her head.

"No, I don't want you to make pizza. I want to go out with you and eat someone else's pizza. Let's meet at The Tin Drum. They have great craft beer." She listened again.

"Yes, seven o'clock will be great. My treat. Yes, if you beat me there, get a table. See you there, Mamma. I love you!"

Magnolia smiled as she put the phone down. A night out with her mother was just what she needed. She'd run home, change clothes, feed the cat, and beat her mom to the restaurant. She'd take a Lyft over, so she could have a couple of beers and not worry about driving home.

A couple of hours later, she and her mom flipped a quarter to see who got the last slice of pizza. Calling heads, Magnolia lost and shoved the pan toward her mom. Elegant and tiny, Pepper Mbele picked up the last piece in her slender fingers, expertly flipped the end over, bent the slice in half like the New York Girl she was, and ate.

Pleased to watch her mom eat, Magnolia swallowed the end of her IPA and signaled the waiter for another by waving the bottle. This would be her third and last. She had early meetings in the morning.

When the waiter arrived with the beer, he picked up the empty pan and the soiled plates on the table. "Dessert?"

"Brownies," Pepper declared firmly. "With mint ice cream."

"Hell, yes," agreed Magnolia.

"You got it." Whisking the dishes away, the waiter headed for the kitchen.

Pepper swished the ice in her iced tea glass then drank. "Feeling better, honey?"

"Oh, Mamma, yes. I feel like the last week or two has washed away. Thanks so much for coming out with me tonight."

"Still this poisoner lady, the Death Cap babe?"

"That's the one. I don't want to talk about her tonight. She's lurking out there, and I can't guess when she will strike next." Magnolia took a swallow of her beer. It was crisp and pleasant, but she wanted to finish it before the ice cream came.

Her mother looked at her over the rims of her glasses. "How will you catch her?"

Sighing, Magnolia set down her half-empty beer. "With any luck, we'll identify her and be able to send out flyers with her picture and IDs on them so that when she shows up somewhere, we'll get a call. Or maybe she'll show up on CCTV somewhere we're watching, although that's the least likely possibility. But we've only got descriptions from the diners' staff and the victims." She drew circles on the table in the condensation from the cold bottle. Struck by an idea, she tapped the bottle on the table.

"Maybe we can get a composite drawing by having the artist work with all the witnesses who've seen her. I'll text and get the police artist on that in the morning." Magnolia pulled her phone out and started tapping rapidly.

The dessert arrived as she finished sending the texts. The ice cream was cold; the giant brownie underneath it was warm. The combination of the two sent little streamers of steam in the air. Taking up a spoon, Magnolia dug in. Her mom did the same. They were regulars at this restaurant, and this was their favorite dessert. The brownies were luscious and chocolatey, and the mint ice cream was a crisp counterpoint. Magnolia thought the vast dessert menu was almost the point of coming to the place. She sighed with pleasure.

"Tell me how this poison works, if this isn't a bad

time. Why is it so deadly?" Her mother looked at her over a spoonful of green ice cream.

Magnolia took some ice cream and licked it gently off the spoon, while figuring out where to start.

"Well, *Amanita phalloides* is the most poisonous of all known mushrooms. Half a mushroom has enough toxin to kill an adult human. Our poisoner seems to be making an extract to add to food to poison her victims rather than putting whole pieces of mushroom in the food. We're not sure where she's getting the amanita mushrooms, but they grow close to certain partner trees. Here in California, for example, *Amanita* is associated with coast live oak and a bunch of hardwoods."

Her mother nodded. "How do you tell it from flu?"

"Symptoms of the death cap mushroom include nausea and vomiting, which come on six to twelve hours after eating. Usually, it looks like the flu. Or food poisoning. The liver and kidneys are affected, which is why the initial symptoms are followed by jaundice, seizures, and coma, which lead to death. Unless the blood is tested for amanita toxins, you can't really tell for almost thirty-six hours, when the jaundice sets in. By then, it's almost too late." Magnolia took a large spoonful of brownie and chewed thoughtfully. "We were lucky that the doctor in the ER felt funny about the whole thing and ordered a tox screen."

Pepper shook her head. "Why on earth would someone be poisoning strangers? It's so bizarre."

"It's like that Tylenol case all those years ago, Mamma. The woman was willing to poison strangers to get her husband. We have no idea about this person's motives. The victims seem random. Until we catch her, we may not know why she's doing it." Magnolia stirred the last bits of ice cream and brownie crumbs together in the bottom of her bowl and scooped them into her mouth. "Until then, I'm not eating anything unusual."

Riding home in the Lyft car, Magnolia thought about how she knew a poisoner was out there but hadn't hesitated to go to her favorite restaurant that night. *That keeps the poisoner in business; people's trust that it can't happen to them.* Despite the hot Sacramento night, she shivered.

6.

Henrietta—real name Lucy, but "Henrietta" was her favorite *nom de crime*—stirred a huge pot of tomato sauce and smiled. This preservation class, operated by the county Cooperative Extension Service, was a gold mine. She was making marinara sauce from some lovely Roma tomatoes she'd found at the market, along with the other ten women in the class. She'd added her special tea—now in a lemon juice bottle—to her kettle under the guise of acidifying the sauce enough to can it in jars. She planned to pass the bottle to the other cooks, creating a lovely flood of poisoned sauces sailing into the community. People shared homemade sauces. She wouldn't have to pick a victim; her cohort in this class would choose them for her. Perhaps one of them would enter the state fair—goodbye, judges!

Ladling the rich sauce into the quart jars she'd already prepared, she happily handed the bottle of "lemon juice" to the woman working next to her and began to cap her jars. The pressure canner was ready for the jars, so she loaded it up and turned to listen to the CES instructor at the front of the class. This was a brilliant idea. She would let her special tea out into the world, and it would choose its victims. She would be miles away when the next set of victims got sick.

She had prepared ten jars; she'd slip her jars in with the contribution to the farmers' market stand run by CES and sneak away. She could do this again in a different county. She chuckled to herself. She was brilliant.

7.

Magnolia's phone rang as she finished her morning Pilates class three days later. She mopped at her sweaty face with a small towel as she listened to the woman on the other end of the phone—a family in Sacramento and two women in Folsom were in the hospital being treated for amatoxin poisoning.

"I'll have a team there shortly," she advised the

woman as she gathered her belongings. "They will take evidence from the victims' kitchens and see what we can find to link these people." She listened again. "Get in touch with Doctor Tompkins at Folsom Mercy," she advised. "He's been treating the initial victims and may have good ideas. Yes. Bye."

Dropping her phone into her bag, she sat on the wood floor to put her sneakers on. She'd go home, shower, and change before going to the Sutter emergency room; showing up in yoga pants and a sweaty T-shirt wasn't strictly professional. She rolled up her yoga mat and put it in its traveling case.

Magnolia sat on a chair at the side of the Pilates exercise room, texting her team from here in the AC rather than sitting in her slowly baking car. She'd need to have three teams moving: one for the family kitchen and one each for the other ladies who'd been affected. Anders could coordinate the field teams while she checked on the victims at the hospital. Sending that memo out to the hospitals and urgent care facilities last month, advising anyone who showed up with resistant vomiting to be tested for amatoxins, had paid off. Maybe they'd caught these folks early enough to save them—unlike poor Sean Kowalski. He'd died waiting for a liver transplant.

When she got to the Sutter ER, a young doctor introduced Magnolia to Sarai Nakai. Sarai's whole family was sick. No one knew why, as everything they had eaten recently had been commercially prepared, except for the salad greens they'd purchased at the farmer's market. Magnolia took notes then texted Anders to check all the food at the Nakai house.

"I have an evidence team at your house currently collecting samples of all the food there, including whatever you were eating for dinner."

"Spaghetti," Sarai interjected.

"Spaghetti," Magnolia echoed, then went on. "It will take them the rest of the night to process the samples, so we won't know what it is until then. But we know you have amatoxins in your bloodstream, so we can begin treating that immediately."

A nurse shouted from a few beds away, and the doctor rushed over. Little Andy Nakai, age eight, was going into convulsions. *It's pretty early in the cycle for this—the poison must have been potent.* Magnolia cursed under her breath.

She decided to go to Folsom Mercy to interview the two other victims.

8.

Magnolia called Anders from the road as she left Folsom. "Anders, all the victims had spaghetti this evening. The Folsom victims got their spaghetti sauce from the farmers' market in Rancho. Check to see if there are jars of home-canned spaghetti sauce at the Nakai house."

"We got it, boss. Spaghetti sauce canned and sold by the Cooperative Extension Service at their booth at the farmers' market. I don't know how the poison got in there, but the residue in the jars tests high for the toxins. I've got the team in Folsom testing, too." Anders popped his gum, the sound clear through the phone speaker.

"Call CES. I'm on my way up there; tell them to hold out any remaining jars of that sauce and to notify anyone who bought it not to eat it!" *Maybe a break at last*, she thought. "Get a list of the CES class members— send evidence teams to their houses to confiscate any sauce they find. If anyone's opened a jar, we need it for testing. The faster we do this, the better."

9.

Lucy was sitting in one of the outdoor cafés on the sidewalk at the farmer's market when she saw the CDPH team show up, their acronym in big yellow letters on the back of their blue windbreakers. She sighed. They'd caught on so fast. She'd been hoping for a week or two of victims before they spoiled this vector. If they had the market, they'd traced it back to the CES class, which meant the Food Pantry jars, too.

She got up and ambled back to where she'd parked her truck, hoping to sneak away before anyone spotted her—only one older woman among many in the crowded market. Glancing over her shoulder, she spotted a tall, lanky man from the team holding a sheet of paper and looking between it and her. He shouted and started toward her.

Running now, her long grey hair streaming out behind her, she moved fast through the crowd. She sped around a booth displaying baskets and, grabbing one corner, pulled the piled baskets down behind her to create confusion and a roadblock.

The tall man was catching up. She grabbed a pint jar of honey off a table and lobbed it at his head, hitting him square in the face. Golden honey dripped down his front and a glass fragment stuck in one cheek. She had stopped him in his tracks. The rest of his team caught up to him as she sprinted away. One quick glance back showed them sitting him down to administer first aid to the cuts on his cheek and forehead.

She ducked into the ladies' room. Someone had left behind a broad-brimmed straw hat and a red jacket. Donning both, she exited out the other bathroom door and headed down the street, strolling toward her truck. She hoped they hadn't identified the truck yet; she'd hate to have to leave it behind.

10.

Anders pointed at the CCTV footage from the

farmers' market and shouted, "That's her. That's the woman who threw the honey at me." He winced and patted the bandage on his forehead. The EMTs had sent him back to the hospital to get stitched up by a plastic surgeon. He'd told Magnolia about the sixty-eight tiny sutures in his face to close up the long gashes from the honey jar in the hope the scars wouldn't be too bad.

The sheriff's deputy running the CCTV footage printed off a clear photo and handed it to Magnolia. "There's your woman. According to facial ID, this is Lucy Sinjin, also known as Henrietta Lackey, Henrietta Lackland, Lucy Simpkins, and Lacy Carmichael. She's wanted in California, Nevada, and Oregon for food tampering and endangering the public; in Orange County, there's a warrant out for her arrest on attempted murder." He leaned back in his chair and drank from his enormous coffee mug.

"What next, boss?" Anders asked Magnolia.

"Unfortunately, at the moment, everything is circumstantial, although her fleeing every time we get close to her indicates guilt. We need to prove she was in the CES class."

"Well, we have evidence someone poisoned that spaghetti sauce. Testing shows the presence of amatoxins in samples taken from class members and the farmers' market. Everything from the Food Pantry has it. The teacher said a woman was passing around a big bottle of lemon juice to acidify the sauce since tomatoes aren't acidic enough anymore to be canned." Anders leaned on the deputy's desk and patted his bandages again.

"That hurt, mack?" the deputy asked sympathetically.

"Yeah, the anesthetic is wearing off. I've got pain pills somewhere, but I have to go home if I want to use them," Anders almost snarled.

"That's a good idea," Magnolia advised him. "Get some rest. We will broadcast this photo far and wide and advise anyone in that CES class, anyone who bought sauce at the farmers' market or from the Food Pantry, to bring it in right away, and if they ate any, to go to the ER right now. Then we have to find her."

11.

Magnolia was briefing a group of sheriffs in Davis when her phone rang. It was her mother. Pepper never called during the day.

"Mamma, what's up?"

"Mags, I don't feel so well. I can't stop throwing up. Can you come help me?"

Magnolia's blood ran cold. "Mamma, what have you been eating?"

"I had spaghetti for lunch and a chef salad from Safeway."

"I'm on my way. Drink as much water as you can

keep down. We'll be going to the emergency room. If you feel like you're going to pass out, call an ambulance. Don't wait for me." Magnolia waited to hear her mom's agreement before she hung up. Quickly telling the team what was happening, she threw her phone in her purse and dashed out the door to her Prius.

When Magnolia arrived, Pepper was sitting on the porch in a camping chair, a bucket near her. "I needed the fresh air," the older woman explained.

"No problem, Mamma." Magnolia was worried—her mom's face was distinctly grey, and her pulse was slow. "Let me gather some samples, and then we'll head off. I think we'll go to Folsom Mercy—that's where the doctors with the most experience are."

In her mom's kitchen, Magnolia grabbed a cloth shopping bag and started loading utensils, food containers, and jars of condiments that were out or showed signs of recent use. In the fridge, she found the bright yellow label of the CES preservation class and cursed. She grabbed the jar of spaghetti sauce and brought it with her.

Back on the porch, Pepper was drowsy and not wholly responsive. Holding onto the bag, Magnolia lifted her diminutive mother into her arms and carried her to the car. After carefully setting her mom in the front seat, she tossed the samples in the back. Placing her emergency light on the roof, she gunned it, siren blazing, as she headed for the hospital.

Once they had her in the emergency room, Dr. Tompkins put Pepper on supportive treatment. Magnolia found herself in the role of patient support—a new role for her. Her mom had called at about 4 p.m. and usually ate her lunch at about 11 a.m., so she could have spent up to five hours being ill before asking for help. Pepper had lapsed into a coma in the car and couldn't tell them any details. Anders had prioritized the samples, and the sauce was positive for amatoxins.

"It's unusually potent stuff—about fifteen percent toxin per ounce of sauce. No wonder our victims have been going down fast," Anders told her.

"We have to catch this bitch," Magnolia snarled. "There's a class at the CES in Davis tonight—I'm going to run over and see what I can see there. Maybe she'll show up to poison more food in the class."

12.

Lucy was happily pickling green beans for canning in quart jars when some new people walked in. She'd chosen this class because it wasn't tomato sauce, and she'd have a chance to start a new vector before the CDPH got wind of it. She had a jar of vinegar adulterated with concentrated amanita juice for pickling. She had her grandma's combination of spices for pickling, as well. The pickles should taste good.

One of the women with some badge on had a professional camera and, after greeting the CES instructor warmly, began taking pictures of the various stages of the class. Lucy tried hard to keep her face away from the camera, picking up the instructions and holding them before her face when the camera was pointed her way.

When the woman came over to take pictures of Lucy's beans, she said, "I did not sign the release for pictures for this class. You may not use any pictures you've taken of me."

The woman sat the camera down on the desk and said, "Don't worry, Lucy. The pictures will only show up in court. I'm here to arrest you on poisoning charges, and I've gathered enough evidence tonight to prove you are the Death Cap Killer."

Still holding the vinegar bottle, Lucy smashed it down on the woman's head, grinned at her, and then ran into the parking lot. She jumped into her Ford F-150 and, tires squealing and smoking, roared onto the frontage road leading to I-80 East.

13.

The salty liquid cascaded down Magnolia's face. Trying not to lick her lips, she grabbed a towel, mopped her face and hair, and threw the towel in an evidence bag. Grabbing the bag and her camera, she ran back out to her Prius.

With her siren on, Magnolia pursued her quarry

over the viaduct and then into Sacramento proper. At the cutoff, she saw the old pickup head onto US 50 rather than I-80, so she figured Lucy must be heading to South Lake Tahoe, her familiar stomping grounds. Driving fast, she caught up to the pickup as they passed Folsom. She was only a few cars behind by El Dorado Hills, where the road started to rise into the foothills.

Suddenly, the pickup swerved into the right-hand lane. The truck slowed, allowing Magnolia's Prius to pull up behind Lucy. Magnolia pulsed the siren and shouted out her open window, "Pull over!"

The pickup continued to drop speed until they were crawling up the hill at 20 miles per hour. *Some high speed chase this was turning out to be!*

When they topped the hill at Bass Lake Road, the pickup gunned it and sped away down the hill toward Cameron Park Drive. Magnolia followed the pickup off the road at Cameron Park Drive and turned north into the small town.

Magnolia watched the pickup turn into the town's commuter airport, plow through the chain link fence, and roar straight across the runway to the taxiway on the other side and into the neighborhood. Magnolia made to follow but had to slam on her brakes and wait while a Cessna 180 made a touch-and-go landing—*someone training, no doubt*—and then followed the truck into the convoluted aviation neighborhood with roads that doubled as taxiways and garages that were also hangars.

Stopping at the first wide intersection, Magnolia looked in the three possible directions for Lucy to have gone and caught sight of red taillights disappearing in the distance. Turning right, she gunned it above the fifteen mph small-town speed limit.

Magnolia realized Lucy must be familiar with the area as she got to the end of the road and faced a brushy wood. The only place to go was down an unpaved access road to the lake. She hoped the footpath was dry enough to drive on.

Dropping her Prius into low gear and turning off the siren, Magnolia pushed through the brush onto the access road and began slowly bumping her way through the woods.

Luck was with her. When she got down the path to the lake, about a mile away, the pickup was bogged in a giant mud puddle.

Lucy sat in the pickup cabin, smoking a cigarette. "Joke's on you, officer," she said. "I just drank the rest of my special tea."

This story is dedicated to my daughter, Jen Brown, who works for the Orange County Health Department in

California. Anything I got right is because of her; anything I messed up is because I dreamed it up instead of checking the Source. I also greatly respect the Cooperative Extension Service, having seen their great service. They just happened to be a convenient vehicle for the bad guy in this story.

The playlist for this story is "R Carlos Nakai Radio" and "Film Scores Radio" on Pandora™.

If you like this book, please leave a review on Amazon or Goodreads. Every honest review, even if it's not a five-star, helps us as independent authors and helps other readers find us.

Look for my witchy romance short stories - the first one is Burning Curtains: A magical short story.

The Cairn's Curse

Michelle Tennant Nicholson

The following story was inspired by an actual mountain biking and hiking trip Michelle, Shannon, Niki, Leigh Anne, and Jennifer experienced in Moab, Utah, in September 2023.

We were supposed to have a good time, you know? A road trip to blow off steam, ride some trails, and enjoy the sheer beauty of the West. What we got instead? A nightmare I wouldn't wish on anyone.

Moab, Utah. I'd seen it in the magazines, dreamt of it, watched videos of all the people hitting those famous red rock trails. We'd already biked our hearts out in Aspen, and the drive from there was stunning. Shannon, my husband, was behind the wheel, and I leaned back listening to Iris, our Husky, panting happily in the backseat. Asheville felt a million miles away, and I was glad for it. We'd met up with our Western North Carolina mountain biking friends Niki, Leigh Anne, and Jennifer in Moab, a rendezvous for one final, unforgettable adventure. And unforgettable it was—just not in the way any of us expected.

The first day, we hit the Raptor Route. I felt free as a bird flying down that trail, wind in my face, Iris barking with excitement as Shannon trailed behind me, calling out, "Wait up, Miche!" I laughed, feeling invincible, like nothing in the world could touch us.

That's when Niki stopped us.

"Guys, look!" she said, her voice a mix of awe and excitement. She was pointing to a perfectly stacked pile of rocks just off the trail. A cairn. Not unusual out here, but something about this one was different. Old. Ancient, even. The way the stones were arranged, you could tell someone had put thought into it. Reverence. It wasn't just a trail marker. It was something more.

"Take a picture of me with it!" Niki called, already reaching for one of the rocks eyeing one to take home, completely unaware of the warning Shannon and I exchanged.

"You sure that's a good idea?" Shannon asked. I swear, my husband has a sixth sense for trouble, but Niki just laughed, tossing a stone in the air and catching it.

"It's fine, just a pile of rocks," she said with a grin,

oblivious to the shiver that crawled up my spine. After the photo, she surreptitiously slipped a small rock into her pocket.

I wish I'd said something about her irreverence. Something more than the casual, "Just don't piss off the rock gods, Nik." Because the moment she touched that stone, something shifted in the air. A low rumble, barely audible, like the earth itself was growling in warning. But none of us really noticed. Not then.

That night, though, everything changed.

The nightmares started small, barely noticeable at first. Niki complained about feeling off. Headaches, nausea—things you could easily chalk up to dehydration or altitude sickness. But then, Iris started acting strange. She was a mountain dog, through and through. Loved being outdoors. But that night, she wouldn't settle. She paced, whining, growling at the shadows like something was lurking just beyond the firelight.

"Probably just coyotes," Shannon said, trying to calm both me and the dog. But I couldn't shake the feeling that something was wrong. The air felt thick, charged, like the calm before a storm.

The next day, we set off on Slickrock trail, hoping to shake off the weird vibes. That's when the accidents started. First, Shannon's bike chain snapped out of nowhere. Then Leigh Anne slipped, twisting her ankle in a way that made her gasp in pain. Jennifer got separated from us for nearly an hour, and by the time we found her, she was disoriented, as if she'd been wandering in a trance.

"Something's not right," I said, but again, we brushed it off. Too many strange things were happening to chalk it up to coincidence, but no one wanted to admit it.

When we woke up the next day we threw caution to the wind. It was a calm Sunday morning (we thought), and since Leigh Anne could still hike on her injured ankle with walking sticks, we decided to hike Mary Jane Slot Canyon. After all, we were on an adventure and time was wasting. The sun was shining and it was time to get our memories made. We'd have to drive back home soon enough. Slot canyons in Utah are beautiful but treacherous—especially when rain was in the forecast. We knew the risks, but none of us were prepared for what was coming.

We'd been hiking for hours, the sun high and relentless, casting sharp shadows across the sandstone walls of Mary Jane Slot Canyon. The air was thick with heat, and the five of us—me, Shannon, Niki, Leigh Anne, and Jennifer—were in high spirits, cracking jokes and admiring the surreal beauty of the narrow, winding canyon.

I glanced up at the sky, noticing a few clouds forming in the distance. "Looks like we might get a little shade," I said, wiping the sweat from my brow.

Shannon nodded, his eyes scanning the canyon

walls. "Let's hope it holds off. We've still got a ways to go before the end of the trail."

Niki was ahead of us, snapping photos with her phone. She turned around and grinned. "Guys, this place is insane! Look at these rock formations!" She pointed to the towering cliffs above, the narrow path between them barely wide enough for us to pass single file. The canyon felt alive, the way the light bounced off the walls, shifting in hues from deep reds to oranges to browns.

It was a place you could get lost in—both figuratively and literally.

As we moved deeper into the canyon, the air grew cooler. The looming cliffs blocked out most of the sunlight now, and the rock underfoot felt smoother, worn down by centuries of water. We knew the end of the trail led to a pool of freezing cold water, a hidden oasis. That's what we'd come for—our reward at the end of the difficult hike.

I noticed the wind picking up slightly, a whisper between the canyon walls. "Hey, guys," I called, trying to keep my voice light but feeling a twinge of unease. "Anyone else feel that wind? It's a bit odd down here."

Leigh Anne, who had been walking quietly for most of the hike as she focused on protecting her ankle from further injury, looked up. "Yeah, it's kinda strange. Isn't the weather supposed to be clear?"

Jennifer, ever the skeptic, shrugged. "We're in the desert. Wind happens."

But Shannon stopped walking and pulled out his phone to check the weather. "Hold up, let me see if there's anything weird going on."

That's when we heard it—the distant roar, like thunder but deeper, more constant. My heart skipped a beat as I looked at Shannon. His face had gone pale.

"Flash flood," he muttered. "We need to move. Now."

Suddenly, the lighthearted mood vanished. Niki turned to look behind us, and I saw her eyes widen. "Oh my God," she breathed. "Look."

We all turned, and there, in the distance, we saw it—a wall of water, mud, and debris rushing toward us, winding through the canyon like some unstoppable force. It was far off, but moving fast. Too fast.

"Run!" Shannon shouted, grabbing my hand as we turned and bolted.

The narrow walls of the canyon made it hard to move quickly. I could feel the panic rising in my chest, every instinct telling me to move faster, but the slick, uneven ground slowed us down. My heart was pounding, adrenaline flooding my system as we sprinted toward higher ground—or at least what we hoped was higher ground.

The roar behind us grew louder, closer. The air was

thick with moisture now, the wind carrying the smell of wet earth. I could hear Niki ahead, her breath ragged, and Leigh Anne's footsteps just behind me. Jennifer was struggling to keep up, and I yelled over my shoulder, "Come on, Jenn, you've got this!"

But the canyon was relentless, twisting and turning, giving us no clear path to escape. Every few steps, the walls seemed to close in tighter, leaving us feeling trapped.

Suddenly, Shannon stopped, pulling me up short. "There!" He pointed to a narrow ledge about six feet up the canyon wall.

"We have to climb," he said, already boosting me up. I scrambled onto the ledge, my hands scraping against the rough rock, heart hammering in my chest. Shannon helped Niki next, then Leigh Anne and Jennifer. He was the last one up. The dog curled in the corner, making the ledge just fine. Four legs are more efficient for climbing! Just as Shannon hoisted himself onto the ledge, the flood roared past us.

The sound was deafening, like a freight train barreling through the canyon. The water churned and thrashed below, a violent mix of mud, rocks, and tree branches. We clung to the rock, our backs pressed against the wall, staring in horror as the canyon floor transformed into a raging river. You could hear the dog whimper occasionally.

For a moment, none of us spoke. We just watched,

stunned, as the water rushed by, carrying away everything in its path. I couldn't even imagine what would've happened if we'd still been down there.

Minutes passed, though it felt like hours, and finally, the flood began to subside. The water level dropped, but the ground below was still covered in thick mud, and debris was scattered everywhere.

Shannon looked at me, his face streaked with sweat and dirt. "We're not out of this yet. We need to get out of the canyon before it happens again."

We climbed down, carefully, slipping on the wet rock. Our dog led the way. The canyon was a mess now—our path back to the car had become a muddy obstacle course. But we had no choice. We had to keep moving.

The hike back was brutal. Every step felt like it took twice the effort, and the mud sucked at our boots and paws, making it hard to find solid footing. The canyon that had seemed so beautiful and inviting earlier now felt like a trap, with every twist and turn bringing new challenges.

But we kept going. One step at a time. Shannon stayed by my side, always looking ahead, his eyes scanning for the next safe path. Niki, Leigh Anne, and Jennifer stayed close, no one saying much. There was nothing to say. We all knew we were lucky to be alive.

When we finally reached the end of the trail, the car was a welcome sight. We collapsed into the seats, exhausted, shaking from the adrenaline and sheer relief.

I wrapped Iris in her favorite blanket as she curled in the car, content to be safe.

I looked out at the canyon one last time, now shrouded in the early evening light. It seemed so peaceful again, as if the flood had never happened. But I knew better. The land out here wasn't something to take lightly. It had its own power, its own rules. We were just visitors, and today, we'd been reminded of that in the harshest way possible.

As we drove away, I glanced at Shannon, then back at the others. "We made it," I said, my voice barely a whisper.

Niki nodded, her face pale but determined. "Yeah, we did. But that was close. Hey—you think that rock I picked up put a curse on us?"

We all laughed, nervous and shaky, knowing how close we'd come. We shrugged it off; still, we couldn't help but wonder if there was a connection between the rock and our unfortunate luck that day.

As the sun set behind us, casting long shadows over the desert, I felt an overwhelming sense of gratitude—for this place, for my friends, and for the fact that we'd survived to tell the story.

We barely made it out of the slot canyon—soaked, freezing, and terrified.

The next morning, we woke and after a big breakfast and tons of organic coffee at Moab Coffee Roasters we decided to visit the Moab Museum around the corner.

Downtown Moab was more like a few streets cornered together. It was hard to decipher between the highway running through the desert and when the city's streets started and stopped. A few food trucks helped us figure out where the heart of the city could be located.

The air in the Moab Museum was cool, a welcome reprieve from the oppressive desert heat outside. The faint hum of the air conditioner buzzed in the background as we strolled through the exhibits. After the adrenaline and terror of the previous days, it felt good to slow down, to take in the history of this place—though I could feel the undercurrent of something still unsettled.

Shannon, Niki, Leigh Anne, Jennifer, and I wandered through the exhibits, each of us lost in our own thoughts. My legs were sore from the brutal hike out of Mary Jane Slot Canyon, and my mind hadn't fully processed the flood, the sheer terror of nearly being swept away by forces we couldn't control. Being here, in this museum, somehow felt grounding. This place, with its relics and stories, connected us to something ancient, something larger than us.

We stopped in front of a large display featuring a detailed map of the Moab area. Above it, a banner read: *The Ancestral Puebloans: Life Among the Red Rocks.*

"Look," Niki said, pointing to a section about the Puebloans. "They lived here thousands of years ago."

The exhibit told the story of the Ancestral Puebloans, a civilization that once thrived in these lands long before pioneers ever set foot on the trails. They were skilled farmers, potters, and builders who had mastered life in the harsh desert environment. Their communities, we learned, flourished here from the 11th to the 12th centuries before they mysteriously disappeared in the 13th century.

"Why did they leave?" Jennifer asked, staring at a replica of an ancient Puebloan clay pot.

Shannon shrugged, flipping through the information about dinosaur prints on a touchscreen nearby. "No one really knows. There are theories about droughts, conflicts, or maybe some kind of environmental catastrophe."

Leigh Anne, who had been unusually quiet since the flood, furrowed her brow. "Or maybe it was something else entirely," she muttered.

I looked at her, sensing the same unease that had been creeping over all of us. We were here, trying to make sense of what we'd experienced. And then, we saw it.

At the far end of the room, past the artifacts and the pottery, was an exhibit on sacred burial grounds. A glass case displayed intricately carved stones and figurines—some of which resembled cairns, stacked rocks like the one Niki had moved on Falcon Flow, the sacred section of Raptor Route. Above the display, a title loomed: *Cursed Cairns and the Sacred Sites of the Ancestral Puebloans.*

Niki stopped dead in her tracks. "Oh no..."

My heart skipped a beat as we all moved closer to the exhibit. The description explained that the Ancient Puebloans believed the land was alive with spirits, and that certain areas, especially burial grounds, were sacred. Cairns, stacked stones often used as trail markers or markers of significance, weren't just random piles of rocks. Some marked ancient burial sites, places where the souls of the dead rested.

"These cairns were often placed by the Ancestral Puebloans to guide the spirits of their deceased, ensuring they found peace in the afterlife," the display read. "It was believed that disturbing these cairns could awaken the spirits, leading to misfortune or a curse upon those who trespassed."

Niki swallowed hard, the color draining from her face. "I didn't know... I didn't realize."

My eyes locked with hers, and a chill ran down my spine. "The cairn. The one you moved."

She nodded slowly. "I thought it was just rocks for a picture. I didn't think it was—"

"A burial marker," Shannon finished, his voice grim. He was staring at the section detailing the consequences of moving cairns in sacred spaces.

It went on to explain that disturbing these markers could bring the wrath of the spirits, often in the form of natural disasters. Flash floods. Accidents. Illnesses.

Misfortune that would follow the person until proper rituals were performed to restore balance.

"We need to do something," Leigh Anne said softly, her voice barely above a whisper. "We need to fix this."

Jennifer, who had been reading in silence, finally spoke. "Look, I don't believe in curses, but after what happened to us in that canyon…" Her voice trailed off as she gestured to the exhibit. "Maybe we should at least try."

I glanced at Shannon, and then at the others. None of us wanted to say it out loud, but it was clear we were all thinking the same thing. There was something real about what we had experienced—something beyond the physical world we knew. We had angered something—something ancient—and we needed to make it right.

The exhibit ended with a note about traditional cleansing rituals, purification ceremonies that could appease the spirits and restore balance. It mentioned that these rituals were still practiced today by the descendants of the Ancestral Puebloans, who lived in the surrounding areas.

"We need to find someone," I said. "Someone who can help us."

Shannon nodded in agreement. "A medicine man. We need to make amends."

Niki, her eyes wide with fear, whispered, "I never should have touched it." She pulled it out of her pocket and showed it to us.

We stood there, silent, letting the weight of it all sink in. The air felt heavy, thick with the stories of the past and the consequences of our actions. We weren't just visitors passing through. We had stepped onto sacred ground, and we had to find a way to set things right.

Before we left the museum, I turned back to the exhibit one last time. The image of the cairns, once just stacks of rocks, now felt alive with meaning. This place, this land, carried ancient stories. Stories that demanded to be heard. And we had just become a part of one of them.

As we stepped out into the scorching desert sun, I knew one thing for sure—we weren't done with this place. Not yet.

Back in Moab, we found a local medicine man—at this point, we were willing to try anything to shake off the literal dark cloud that seemed to follow us.

He listened as we told him everything. The cairn, the accidents, the storm.

"You've disturbed the spirits," he said calmly, his eyes sharp, knowing. "These lands are sacred. The rocks are more than just markers. They guard the ancestors. Taking one without respect has consequences."

He instructed us to return the stone and perform a purification ritual. We gathered sage, tobacco, and water from a nearby spring, as he'd instructed, and headed back to the canyon with him by our side to instruct us.

The air was thick with tension as the medicine man

led us to the cairn. He began the smudging ceremony, the scent of burning sage filling the air, as he chanted words in a language older than time itself. The smoke curled around us, and for the first time in days, I felt a strange calm wash over me.

Niki returned the rock, placing it carefully where she had found it. Tears streamed down her face, her hands shaking as she whispered apologies into the wind.

The medicine man made an offering of tobacco, scattering it to the earth, and then spoke a prayer to the spirits. His voice was steady, filled with reverence and power:

"Great Spirit of the Earth and Sky,

Hear our voices as we come before you in humility.

We acknowledge the sacred land on which we stand,

The home of the ancestors, whose spirits dwell here.

Ancient ones, guardians of this sacred place,

We offer our deepest apologies for the disturbance we have caused.

We did not know, and we ask for your forgiveness."

As he finished, the air around us seemed to shift. The heaviness lifted, replaced by a sense of peace. The medicine man nodded, satisfied. "The spirits have accepted your apology. But remember—respect the land and its guardians. Always."

We didn't need to say it out loud. We knew we had survived something ancient, something beyond us. The land had spoken, and we had listened. Now, it was time to go.

As we started the drive out of Moab, the familiar red rock formations seemed softer, more welcoming somehow. I knew we were leaving something behind—but we were also taking something with us, something we hadn't expected to find.

We stopped at an overlook just before heading out of the park. It was the same spot where we'd taken pictures on the way in, back when we were just excited mountain bikers ready for an adventure. We stood there, looking out over the vast expanse of red desert and towering mesas, the same land that had felt so ominous just a day ago. But now, there was a quiet beauty to it, a balance restored.

"I guess it wasn't just about the rocks, huh?" Niki said, her voice breaking the stillness.

We all laughed, but there was truth in her words. It wasn't about the rocks—or the trail, or even the canyon. It was about respect, about understanding that this land held something far older and far greater than us. Something we could never truly possess, only visit.

The medicine man's words echoed in my mind: *The land is alive, and we are but guests.*

As we stood there, taking it all in, I found myself feeling grateful—not just for surviving, but for learning. For seeing the world in a way I hadn't before. I'd come to Moab for a ride, but I was leaving with something much deeper.

We all left Moab changed. What started as a fun adventure had turned into a lesson we wouldn't soon forget. We'd disturbed something ancient, something powerful, and we were lucky to have escaped with our lives. Even now, back in Asheville, I can still feel the weight of what happened. Iris, too—she's calmer, but every now and then, I catch her staring at something I can't see, her eyes following shadows that don't exist.

Maybe it's nothing. Maybe it's just the wind.

Or maybe... the spirits are still watching.

Back in Asheville, life moved on. The chaos of Moab felt like a distant memory, but it never really left me. Not fully. It was there in small moments—the way Iris would pause and sniff the air on our walks, or how Shannon and I would exchange quiet glances when we passed by a trail marker. The land had left its mark on us, and we were better for it.

Niki stopped taking photos with rock formations, of course, but every time she hit the trails, you could see it in her—an awareness, a kind of quiet reverence for the ground beneath her tires. Leigh Anne's ankle healed, but she, too, walked with a bit more caution, a little more respect for the paths she took. Jennifer, ever the skeptic, never said much about it, but I could tell she felt it too.

One day, Shannon, Iris, and I decided to take a quiet hike up in the Blue Ridge. It was one of those perfect mountain mornings—crisp air, the sun breaking through the trees, the world just waking up. As we walked, I spotted something up ahead on the trail.

A small cairn. Neatly stacked, each rock balancing perfectly on the one below it.

I paused, staring at it for a moment. And then, with a smile, I carefully stepped around it, making sure it stayed exactly as it was. Shannon looked at me, and I could see the understanding in his eyes.

The trail ahead was long, winding through the trees and disappearing into the mountains. And for the first time in a while, I felt at peace with where we'd been—and where we were headed. Because I knew now, wherever we went, we'd tread lightly.

We were, after all, just visitors.

Michelle Tennant Nicholson is an award-winning writer, publicist, and storyteller. She's the author of *The Dairy Princess Chronicles: My Journey to W.R.I.T.E. the Trauma*, where she shares how she overcame trauma, found happiness, and helps others do the same. A former professional whitewater raft guide, Michelle is now a mountain biker and proud mom to a Yakutian Laika.

Want more stories? Sign up for her email list to read her true crime thriller and follow her column, *Mental Injury Is Not Mental Illness: From Fight, Flight, Freeze to Flow,* on Psychology Today. Sign up here.

https://mailchi.mp/7fd07c96fedb/michelle-tennant-author-newsletter

What Satisfies Hunger
Amy Rivers

My name is Sharon Ruttledge, and I have an unhealthy relationship with food. If I'd ever bothered going to Overeaters Anonymous, I imagine these are the words I'd have said. Truth is, I'm just hungry. Hungry? No, more like compelled to eat. All the time.

I grabbed a clean plate after adding to my stack of empties, ignoring the hateful look on Michelle's face. I'd insisted on the buffet over my sister's protests, knowing that I'd get my money's worth and she would not.

"I can't believe you went back for more. Don't you ever stop eating?" Michelle had been done for quite some time. I ignored her and went back to my food.

This particular dive, with its bare bulbs and slightly suspicious smells, was one of my favorites. The food was overly salty and just shy of spoiling. I couldn't get enough. My hunger never abated. Every few minutes, I glanced at the host podium. When the expression on the host's face shifted from nervousness to irritation, I would head home.

I plucked a grain of rice off the dirty tabletop and popped it in my mouth, amused to see Michelle turn an unattractive shade of green.

"Jesus, Sharon. Do you have to eat like an animal?" It had been years since Michelle even attempted to hide her disgust with my eating habits.

"You don't have to stay," I said, shoveling another forkful of rice into my mouth, as more grains cascaded to the table below.

A flash of hurt crosses Michelle's face, but it's quickly replaced with a scowl. I've been immune to Michelle's constant need for attention for a long time. She doesn't really want to be here, but she hates being dismissed.

You're a fat cow, Sharon. The voice in my head was always louder when Michelle was around. That's part of the reason I avoid her. The other part? I hate her. Ever since Daddy died, Michelle and I had done everything we could to forget we were related. It was easy, of course, because we aren't. Michelle's mother died shortly after giving birth, leaving Daddy alone and unprepared to care for a baby. When he met my mama, it didn't much matter that she had a bastard child so long as she could change a diaper and make a decent meal.

Daddy loved Michelle. She was the only person I'd ever seen him show any affection for and she'd grown mean because of it. Whatever closeness we'd had when we were little was erased by an ugly, vicious need for Daddy's attention. Michelle was convinced that Daddy loved me more.

Michelle didn't have the faintest notion about the ways her daddy had *loved* me. No amount of food would ever erase the feel of his hot breath on my belly, his hands where no father's hands should ever go. Mama had run off without even saying goodbye, leaving me in Daddy's care. The three of us: me, Daddy, and Michelle.

I stuffed another piece of chicken in my mouth.

"Why are we here, Michelle?" I snapped, ready to be done with her for the day. I hadn't seen Michelle since Daddy died and I hadn't missed her.

"Daddy's lawyer called a few days ago." I stopped eating, waiting for the inevitable bad news. "They've finally settled Daddy's estate. He left me some insurance money."

"Big surprise," I muttered, though I didn't really care. I knew Daddy wouldn't leave me a dime. His death was enough for me, but my need for food kept me feeling shackled.

Michelle's eyes turned dark as midnight. "Actually, Daddy left you the house."

I choked. Was this a joke? The house we grew up in was little more than a shack surrounded by a copse of dead trees. Every bad thing that had ever happened to me, happened within those walls. Even in death, Daddy added to my nightmares and heartache.

"I don't want it."

Her cheeks turn nearly purple with rage. "He *should* have left it to me."

"Well, you can have it," I say between bites, but I'm a little bit fascinated by how quick she is to anger today.

"You can sell it if you want to. The land is probably worth something." The wolfish look on Michelle's face sent shivers down my spine. "Aren't *you* lucky he's dead."

"You have no idea."

Now, I'd spent many an hour picturing ways to kill Daddy. Sometimes, when he was on top of me, it was the only thing that kept me from screaming and waking Michelle up. Why I'd spent any energy protecting her from that vile, disgusting monster is beyond me. She was just as bad. Worse even. It wasn't hard to figure out Daddy's style of violence. It was right in your face. Michelle's a schemer.

That being said, I'd been shocked when I'd come home to discover Daddy's bloated body, an empty whiskey bottle wrapped in his fingers. Everyone knew Daddy was a drunk, so his death wasn't unexpected. But something never sat right with me about the way he looked that night.

Not that I had let it bother me long.

Michelle had been living in town for two years when Daddy died, and she rarely visited, leaving Daddy to his drink and me to my food. I'd always been a plump child, but when Daddy's nighttime visits began, eating became my refuge. As I grew fatter, I hoped he'd find me as repulsive as everyone else did and leave me alone. No such luck. Instead, my only pleasure in life came from bread and sugary sweets and all things fried. I didn't care what I looked like. I just wanted to eat until I died. Some days I hoped the end would come sooner than later. Today was one of those days.

"Why can't you take the house?" I asked, though I couldn't imagine why she'd want the dump. I'd filled a large soup bowl with mashed potatoes and gravy. The brown liquid oozed over the side and onto the plate. Grabbing a roll from the mountain I'd amassed nearby, I began sopping up the potatoes and gravy.

"I just can't," Michelle started, and something in her tone put me on high alert. "I could buy it from you. You know, for cheap. Since we're sisters." If I'd learned one thing, it was that Michelle never did anything out of family loyalty. I didn't want the land or the house, but I decided right then and there I'd never let her have it. I stared at my sister in stony silence.

I raised a brow. "You're probably right. I'll just sell it." That she caught my implied *not to you* was evident on her face.

"He always liked you better than me," she hissed. I couldn't help but laugh at how far off the mark she was.

"Fine." Michelle's face was turning an even uglier shade of purple. "Here." She pushed an envelope across the table to me. "It's all yours."

###

He left the house to me with instructions never to sell it. Like his wishes would stop me from doing whatever I wanted to. But I still wondered why.

Standing in front of the house, I suppressed the urge to vomit. After Daddy died, I'd taken the money I'd been stashing away and moved into town. My apartment was run-down and tiny, but it was safe, a far cry from the tormenting home of my childhood.

Leave my house alone, you bitch. Daddy's voice still echoed in my head. When I'd seen his dead body, the first thing I thought was how I'd never have to hear that horrible sound again. Wrong. From that first night, Daddy's words taunted me. I'd moved, thinking the distance would make it stop. It didn't. Daddy's ghost wasn't interested in haunting a house. Even from the grave, his focus was all on me.

"It's my house now," I said loudly, trying to muster some courage.

I'd taken two steps forward when a gust of cold wind blew through the trees and the front door opened with a bang, making me jump.

"Dammit." I was so jittery my teeth were beginning to chatter. It was infuriating how that bastard still made me shake in my boots.

Gravel crunched beneath my shoes as I inched toward the house, mocking myself for being such a baby, but unwilling to move any faster. Something pulled at my collar, urging me to turn around and leave forever. But if Michelle wanted this place, I was determined to tear it down. And she sure as shit wasn't going to get the money for the land either.

When I walked inside the house, nothing had changed. I don't know what I was expecting. No one had been inside since shortly after Daddy's death. But the lack of dust and the papers spread casually on the table gave me the creeps. I could almost imagine Daddy walking through the door demanding his supper.

That's not all I want. I closed my eyes, begging a God I'd never prayed to before to release me from this torment. Daddy had been a loud man, and I was never surprised to hear his bellowing voice in my mind. But this low, seductive murmur brought with it an explosion of adrenaline and a desperate need to escape.

I ran to my car, launching myself behind the wheel,

my heart threatening to explode in my chest. I looked back at the lonely house, sitting in the clearing with the front door still wide open.

Something inside me snapped. I'd spent the last twelve years of my life being tortured by Daddy and despised by Michelle. My mother had abandoned me without a thought. I'd be damned if I was going to spend a minute longer than I had to dealing with what was left of that wretched life.

I got out of the car long enough to close the front door, then drove home. When I got there, I dialed up the first realtor in the phone book. After making myself a heaping pot of spaghetti, I ate until I passed out.

I admit, I expected it to take a while for the realtor to get back to me, so imagine my surprise when she called me two days later to set up a showing.

"The client is really interested, so I think we should try and close the deal quickly." Her voice hinted at a desire to get rid of this property and the person attached to it. I wasn't offended.

We agreed to meet in the early afternoon, and as the hour drew near I got nervous, Daddy's voice ringing in my head: *Don't you dare sell my house! You hear me, girl?* I left a little early so I could stop by the Krispy Kreme. I was licking at the remnants of a dozen glazed donuts stuck to my fingers when the realtor arrived with her client, a birdlike woman in a long flowered skirt.

"This is Wanda," the realtor introduced us. I took Wanda's hand in mine, imagining that if I squeezed, I would break her. "Wanda is looking for a cabin in the woods. But I told her the house isn't in great shape."

"Nonsense," Wanda said. Her voice was wispy and frail, but her tone was confident. "I can fix anything."

I opened the front door to reveal a disaster area. The living room, which had been neat, if neglected, only two days ago looked as though a tornado had blown through. The old sofa was slashed, the coffee table overturned and it looked like someone had keyed the walls.

I cringed as the realtor gasped. "What did you do?" Her tone was filled with accusation and disgust.

"I didn't do anything!" My voice was screechy. The sensation of fingers gripping my shoulder had returned and I felt panic sweeping over me in waves.

Only Wanda seemed at ease. "Well, it's a bit of a mess, but I'm sure I can get it cleaned up." The look on the realtor's face was priceless. I'm sure we were both wondering where this crazy lady came from.

Get that bitch out of my house. His voice tore into my already addled mind like a dagger. My breathing became ragged and I grabbed desperately at the wall for support.

"Are you OK?" the realtor asked me, but her tone rang with unfiltered irritation.

"Fine," I said, trying to regulate my breathing. "It's just a little dusty in here."

Meanwhile, Wanda floated from room to room with exclamations of "ooh" and "wonderful." By the time she returned to the front room, my nerves were completely shot. I began backing toward the door, Daddy's voice screaming *GET HER OUT* so loudly it was making me nauseous. Luckily, the realtor's discomfort was nearly as bad as my own and she said, "Well, I guess we'd better head back to town."

"Good," Wanda said, her smile revealing yellowing teeth. "I'm quite sure I want to buy this property."

Dumbfounded, the realtor ushered Wanda back to the car, leaving me alone on the front step.

I turned and looked at the house. Daddy's voice had died down, allowing space for every bad memory to resurface. My chest hurt and, for a moment, I hoped I might die of a heart attack right then and there. Soon, Daddy's voice came back with a vengeance. *Don't let that crazy bitch have the house.*

"Why?" I said out loud, wondering if talking back to a ghost meant I was going crazy.

Just do as you're told. His voice was louder, more insistent. But I heard something else.

Fear.

The only two emotions I couldn't recall Daddy ever showing were happiness and fear. Rationally, I suppose he must have felt both of those at some point in his life, but even with Michelle, I'd never seen him happy, though he clearly felt something for her. And he wasn't afraid of anything. Until now.

I can't say why I didn't just leave. Maybe it was the fear in Daddy's voice that emboldened me. But I got up and walked back into the house. The only time I'd ever heard even a hint of *concern* in Daddy's voice was when it came to Michelle. A thought nagged at the back of my mind. Why would Daddy leave me the house? And then it hit me. He was protecting something, or someone.

I made a beeline to Michelle's old room.

It had been years since I'd set foot in this room. The first thing that struck me was how clean and organized her room was compared to the rest of the house. Everything was in its place, as if she'd taken nothing with her when she moved out. Was that possible? The bedding was pristine. While the rest of us lived in filth, it looked like daddy made sure his real daughter was well taken care of. I got angry and with my anger came hunger. An intense, burning hunger deep in my gut. I was about to close the door when I spotted the tiniest glint of something shiny poking out behind a nightstand in the corner.

A sense of foreboding and impending revelation waged war on my resolve. Finally, I stooped to pick up the object. It was wedged firmly in a hole in the floorboard—I'm surprised I even noticed it. When I finally got it unstuck, a memory hit me like a lightning strike. It was a pendant—a bird with its wings broken off.

"Your mama was wearing that the day she died." I whipped around. Michelle was standing in the doorway. Cold fear gripped my heart. "She always told Daddy you were her little bird." Michelle took a step toward me. I stumbled back into the wall. The fear in my heart became a raging heat. Pain shot down my arm and my chest tightened. I sank to my knees. *Can't you do anything right?* Daddy's voice was a low growl in my head. *I left the house to you so she'd be safe.*

"You killed my mama," I croaked through gritted teeth. "And Daddy knew."

"He wasn't *your* daddy," Michelle spat. "He was mine! After your mama was gone he gave you all his attention, and I realized what a selfish bastard he was. Then, last year, he told me he was leaving you the house. Said he was *protecting* me. I got rid of him."

She grinned.

I collapsed, emptying the contents of my swollen stomach onto the floor in great heaves.

Resting my head on the wooden floor, I could now see that some critter had been chewing away at something hidden behind the wall panel where the pendant had been wedged. A fleck of white caught my attention and I reached a trembling finger out to touch it. I screamed as a piece of bone rolled toward me, dislodged by my shaking hands. I pulled myself up against the wall and tried to calm my breathing.

For the first time in forever, I was decidedly not hungry. Michelle had left the room, and I rummaged around in my pocket for my phone. Pain radiated through my chest and down my arm, making breathing difficult. I could hear Michelle's footsteps down the hall. I dialed 911. When the dispatcher answered, I whispered, "My sister is trying to kill me. Please send help." Then I shoved the phone underneath me with the line open.

I could still hear the dispatcher speaking, but the sound was muffled. I moaned loudly, hoping to disguise the sound long enough that they might be able to trace the call. I had the feeling I wouldn't be walking out of this house, but I'd be damned if I didn't take Michelle, and Daddy, down with me.

You stupid whore! Daddy's voice rang through my skull.

I would have smiled, but my chest was so tight I was finding it hard to control my body. I looked up to see Michelle stalking toward me, laughing cruelly.

"I brought you a snack since you're always so starving, little sister. " She knelt down next to me, setting a bucket of greasy fried chicken on the floor. The smell made my stomach turn.

"No," I croaked, but the sound died in my throat as Michelle pulled some chicken off the breastbone and shoved it into my mouth. I began to choke. I tried spitting it out, but Michelle kept pushing more in, bones and all.

Michelle's laughter was cut short by the sound of a siren in the distance. We looked at each other–me struggling against impending death, her still as stone. As my vision began to fade around the edges, I realized that this might just be the best thing that had ever happened to me in this house.

Amy Rivers is an award-winning novelist, as well as the Director of Writing Heights Writers Association. She was named 2021 Indie Author of the Year by the Indie Author Project. Her psychological suspense novels incorporate important social issues with a focus on the complexities of human behavior. Amy was raised in New Mexico and now lives in Colorado with her husband and children. Find her novels with your favorite retailer.

WINTEROVERS
Kara Smith

lice clung to the cargo netting, her stomach crawling its way up out of her throat. She didn't know how much more she could take. The LC-130 Hercules aircraft was packed to capacity with supplies, and the last group of winter-overs to arrive for the season. On its final approach to the icy expanse of the South Pole, the bird dropped, dove, and shook wildly as if it were trying to escape some unseen predator. An empathetic co-traveler, bundled up so only his icy blue eyes were showing, handed Alice a barf bag just in time. All she could think was, *How did I get myself into this?* Which was a ridiculous question because she knew exactly how she had gotten herself into this.

* * *

Sitting at her desk table that doubled as her kitchen counter, Alice contemplated what she wanted to do next. Her Sprinter Van had been her home for the past four years, and her savings had now gone completely dry. She stared at her computer screen, torn between writing another piece on California Coastal Camper living or applying at a local coffee shop in Santa Barbara for a month or two to fund her continued travels. Anything to avoid going back to mundane office life.

Her phone buzzed. The caller ID showed Max Dancy, one of the associate editors for a large investigative magazine and Alice's Harvard classmate from over a decade prior. Max usually reached out when he wanted something, like a contact or a lead, and although against her better judgement, she always answered his call in case it might lead to a real opportunity. She inserted her wireless earbud.

"Hi Max, how are you?" Alice greeted him cheerfully, masking her reservations. Stepping out of the van for a breath of fresh salty sea air, she looked out at the Pacific Coast Highway, wondering if ignoring the call might have spared her some pride. She stretched her long tan and toned limbs then tucked her wavy hair into a messy bun, preparing for what she expected to be mental gymnastics.

"Hey Alice. I need a favor."

Typical. Don't say yes unless this favor comes with

compensation. "You're into freelance travel journalism now, right?" Max asked.

Debating internally whether her sporadic and largely unpublished writings qualified her to use such a title, Alice hesitantly replied, "Been on the road for four years, picking up jobs here and there. So, yeah, travel journalism, I guess."

"I had a journalist lined up for a six-month imbedded position who broke his leg, and now I need someone else."

"Max, why are you calling me? You have others on your staff."

"Because nobody else will take it."

Alice was quiet for a moment, wondering where in the world he wanted to send her. "Where is it?"

"Do you like the cold? I'll make it worth your while, promise!"

Alice was regretting saying yes to Max as she puked into the paper bag again. The massive aircraft, equipped with skis instead of wheels, finally came to a shuddering stop at Jack F. Paulus Skiway.

"'There is no such thing as a small miracle in aviation,'" she whispered. The man across from her gave her an odd look. "Mark Twain," she said, wiping off the remnants of vomit with her sleeve.

His odd look turned into annoyance. *Not a fan apparently.* Alice stood up, grabbed her pack from under her seat, and lined up behind her new colleagues to walk out the back of the aircraft. The air instantly stung when it hit her face and slyly stole her breath as it poured through the fuselage.

Waiting for their arrival were approximately thirty people bundled up in red parkas, standing next to the PAX terminal of the Skiway. The group was lined up with their gear and carefully packed pallets to load onto the plane in a quick turnover amidst the blowing snow and subzero temperatures.

Between whips of snow, Alice could just make out in the dim light all of Amundsen-Scott South Pole Station and the associated scientific buildings, including the IceCube Neutrino Observatory, clustered within one square mile of the Skiway. Alice made a mental note for her story that would be published in one of the largest investigative magazines in the world.

This was the biggest publication she had ever landed, but it would cost her six months of her life and her tan, all while stranded at the bottom of the earth. But deep down she hoped it would be worth it.

Trudging towards the main building from the landing strip, the dark grey structure loomed above the ice. From this angle, it resembled a long rail car. As Alice walked towards her new home, the departing tenants of this remote outpost hurried onto the plane, efficiently loading the pallets and themselves before the offloading crew could even reach the station. Climbing up the stairs, Alice looked back just in time to see the plane taxiing along the ice.

It is well known to anyone who ventures to the bottom of the Earth that in the summer season at the pole, there is the ability to hop a flight out if need be, but in the winter, roughly February to November, the pole is shrouded in complete darkness and the temperatures are so cold a plane's gasoline would freeze attempting to reach the station.

There is no turning back now.

Alice entered the station behind the others through the landing deck's double doors. All of her fellow travelers seemed to know their way around and were warmly greeted by other scientists and staff as they shed their jackets, stowing them in the coat room before dispersing to their assigned tasks.

While hanging up her coat, Alice stole a glance into the adjacent conference room. Seated at the large conference table was a rugged-looking man, engrossed in a game of cricket on the screen above the official-looking table. His dark brown wavy hair matched his beard, and he still wore his issued snow bibs over his thermal top, suspenders clinging tightly over his broad shoulders, suggesting he had just come in from the cold.

"Oi, ya flaming galah! That was unheard of!" he argued with the TV in a distinct Australian accent.

"Excuse me," Alice said softly, startling the man who blushed when he turned and saw her standing in the doorway. "I am supposed to be meeting," she dug around in her pants pocket for her phone, unlocked it, and pulled up the name, "Ryder Wilson, the Safety Director. Would you know where I could find him?"

"That's me," he said, tapping the control panel in front of him to turn off the television. "It's a banger of a match, shame I won't finish it." He walked towards Alice and motioned her to move out of the doorway. "G'day, Mrs. Lewis. Sorry for the delay"

"Just Ms.," she corrected him. "And don't those matches last for days?"

"Righto, let's get you sorted." He picked up one of her bags and started walking down the long hallway.

Alice stepped in and grabbed her bag out of his hand. "I've got it," she insisted, unwilling to let him do the work for her. His lack of conversation was coupled with his brisk pace, power walking towards their destination, past office spaces, lab rooms, stairwells that looked like they led to the bottom floor, and a vast collection of memorabilia plastering the walls.

They turned right near the end of the long hallway, going through a single door and making their way halfway down another narrower hallway with many doors. Ryder stopped in front of one bearing Alice's name on a paper slip, which looked to have been hastily shoved into the name plate spot. He unlocked the door and handed Alice the key.

"This here's gonna be yer berthing for the next few months. Got myself a master key in case you misplace yers. Showers are down yonder to yer left. Gotta keep an eye on yer water usage, remember the spiel from the safety briefing before you set off? If ya don't recollect, it's in the binder on yer desk, just over there." He pointed into the tiny tin can of a room, which consisted of a government-issue armoire, a raised twin bed, and a desk opposite the bunk in matching camel laminate. The size of the room was barely half of her Sprinter Van.

"Thanks." She took the keys from his hand, entered the small windowless room, and threw her bag on the bed.

"I would like to interview you fir—" she started to say before turning around to see Ryder had already left. "—st... when you have moment," she finished despite his absence as she picked up her other bag. She poked her head out the door and looked in both directions down the empty passageway, but he was nowhere to be seen.

"Okay, then. Nice to meet you too," she said quietly to nobody.

She unpacked what little she had brought, then reviewed the safety binder front to back. After trying to commit to memory the lay of the facility from the map, she made her way to the main dining hall where she was supposed to meet up for newcomers orientation at 14:00 sharp.

The galley, which stretched longer than it was wide, was empty. *Am I early?* She checked her watch before grabbing an upside-down chair from a nearby table and taking a seat. *Maybe I'm the only newcomer.*

After admiring the windows adorned with colorful pictures to trap in the warmth and stave off the impending darkness of the coming days, she began jotting down notes on her electronic tablet about her journey so far:

Landing was a doozy.

Scientists don't appreciate Mark Twain quotes. Room small and isolating.

Head of safety, a complete asshole.

"I prefer to be called Mr. Asshole," Ryder said from over her shoulder.

"CHRIST!" Alice nearly fell backwards in her chair. "Not cool."

Ryder pulled down a chair and sat in it backwards, settling directly across from Alice.

"Alright, listen up," he stated bluntly as he crossed his hands on the table. "Yer here 'cause yer editor, Max Dancy, called in a favor with the big bosses over at the National Science Foundation. Apart from that, yer just another body, gobbling up resources and wasting our time down here."

Although taken aback by the frosty reception, Alice maintained her composure. She responded with the first thought that came to her mind: "What are you hiding?"

Ryder smirked. "Ah, you journos always stirrin' the pot, aren't ya? Summertime's full of yer type, but us winter folk don't have time for yer shenanigans. There are fifty-one souls on this station this winter and they all have a job to do, that doesn't include being harassed by you."

"Fifty-two souls," she corrected him. "You left me out."

"That's 'cause you don't chip in to keep this place running and the mission on track, and that's exactly why I'm not keen on having ya here," he hit back.

"I was assigned here to write a story about life down here in total darkness, and that's what I am going to do. Either you can help me, or I can figure things out for myself. But I have a job and I intend to do it," Alice said with no waiver in her tone.

Ryder stared at her skeptically. "You can write about whatever ya like but I won't be subjecting the staff on this station to yer interference." He got up and was almost to the door when he turned around and pulled a radio from his back pocket. "Keep this on and charged at all times. You will be called by name." He tossed the radio at Alice before turning to walk away. She caught it without breaking eye contact.

"So was that the newcomers' orientation?" She yelled to Ryder the door swinging shut behind him. He didn't respond.

Alice returned to her berthing and pulled out her laptop, immediately initiating a video call with Max. It rang multiple times before Max's face appeared on the screen, the Chrysler Building and the rest of the NYC skyline looming behind him.

"What the hell did you send me down here for?" Alice said without preamble. "They don't want me here."

"Oh, good, you made it! What time is it there?" Max asked, not showing any concern with the attitude she was emanating through the screen. "Is it as cold as they say?" he asked.

"Yeah, it's cold and then some. I've barely been here two hours, and I've already hit a wall with the man I am supposed to coordinate my interviews through," she said, nearly snarling, but keeping her voice at a whisper so nobody would hear her through the thin walls.

"Yeah, about that..." Max hesitated. "I know you thought you were going down there to do a documentary piece, but there has been a change in plans."

"What do you mean?" Alice asked, a sense of unease creeping over her.

"A few months back, a tip came through of some

very strange behavior by the returning personnel the last two seasons."

"What do you mean by strange?"

"Over seventy of the scientists who have been down there for the winter have either left their spouses, quit their jobs, or outright disappeared."

"Oh, come on, Max. That's over eighty percent of the personnel. There is no way that's possible."

"Well, my sister made a pretty compelling case when her husband of fifteen years decided to walk out just days after returning last year. I need you to find out what's going on down there."

Alice sat back, shaking her head in disbelief. "What other information do you have?"

"The scientists who didn't go crazy have stayed tight-lipped about their colleagues. So the only option was to send someone down there."

Alice was intrigued, maybe the next six months wouldn't be so boring after all.

"I'll do my best," was all she could say, and she shut her computer without saying goodbye.

Alice paced back and forth in her 100-square-foot digs, her mind racing with uncertainty.

What the hell am I going to do? This alien environment, surrounded by strangers who likely harbored significant secrets, was a far cry from what she thought this assignment would be.

Collapsing onto her bed, exhaustion from the

journey washing over her, Alice gazed up at the ceiling adorned with a makeshift galaxy of glow-in-the-dark stars left behind by the previous occupant. She reached up one long leg and switched off the light with her foot. She fell asleep staring up at the stars.

* * *

KNOCK KNOCK KNOCK

Alice awoke without opening her eyes. "Okay, alright! I'll move the damn van!" she mumbled. Then she remembered she wasn't in her van. She looked around and noticed the galaxy above was no longer glowing, meaning she had been asleep for quite some time. Her stomach growled confirming her suspicions.

"Alice, git up." She recognized Ryder's deep Aussie accent and instantly cringed at the thought of answering the door. She peeled herself up and reached for the handle anyway.

"'But the fact is I was napping, and so gently you came rapping, and so faintly you came tapping, tapping at my chamber door,'" she said quietly while she opened her door.

"Poe was off his rocker, mate." Ryder gave Alice a squint-eyed glare, his face twisting in confusion. "And yer no different. Ya skipped dinner and brekkie, and missed yer checkup at the doc's, and failed to answer yer radio. I may not be yer biggest fan, but I gotta make sure ya stay alive down here. Sort yerself out and get down to the med bay, pronto."

Alice looked over at her radio on the desk. Ryder leaned in, grabbed it, and swapped out the battery.

"Yeah, righto boss, I'll sort it out straight away," she said in her best Australian accent, giving him a casual two finger salute from her eyebrow.

Ryder rolled his eyes before he shut the door on Alice, nearly missing her nose. "Yeah, he's definitely warming up," Alice said to herself.

Alice looked at her laptop to check the time: 10:38.

She had slept straight through to the next morning, a testament to the toll of her global travels. Unsurprised by this, she hastily donned a fresh set of clothes, opting to postpone her shower. On reaching the med bay, she was instructed to wait outside. Seated in a chair, she observed a few others passing by until the door adjacent to her opened, revealing a short woman in a white lab coat peering around the corner.

"Alice?" the older woman inquired, pushing up her horn-rimmed glasses and consulting her clipboard. "You're my last check-in for the season. Please, come in," she warmly invited.

Alice entered the med bay, stealing a quick glance at the clipboard in the woman's hand. It contained a roster of all fifty-two station occupants. The doctor placed the clipboard on the counter next to her desktop, arms reach from where Alice was directed to take a seat. The room was spacious, with multiple beds separated by curtains and various types of medical equipment neatly stored in adjacent cabinets.

"Nice to meet you, Alice. I'm Dr. Chen, but everyone calls me Dr. Diane," she introduced herself, extending her hand for a handshake, which Alice reciprocated. Dr. Diane had an uncomfortably firm grip.

"I apologize for missing my earlier appointment; I overslept," Alice admitted timidly.

"Not uncommon at all, given your journey. You're not the first, and certainly won't be the last. Don't let Ryder guilt-trip you. Besides, last night was the movie marathon; not many people were up and about too early," Dr. Diane reassured her.

"Oh, what movies?" Alice asked with a slight touch of FOMO washing over her.

"That would be *The Thing from Another World*, *The Thing* made in 'eighty-two, and then the newer one from 2011. It's a longstanding tradition to stay up late and watch them after the last flight departure for the season."

Alice sat quietly, contemplating the dark ironic detachment involved in the tradition, considering the movies' themes of paranoia, isolation, and the fear of the unknown. The newest movie was based in Antarctica, and the station ends up being destroyed at the hands of aliens. Alice's FOMO evaporated.

The doctor rose from her seat and headed towards

one of the metal cabinets behind her, where she inadvertently dropped her keys. Seizing the opportunity of distraction, Alice retrieved her phone from her cargo pocket and snapped a picture of the clipboard, swiftly returning her phone to her pocket before Dr. Diane had located the correct key to open the cabinet.

Dr. Diane handed Alice a bottle of supplements. "These are your vitamin D supplements. Be sure to take them daily," she instructed, leading Alice to a phlebotomy chair for a blood draw.

"I hope you're not afraid of needles; I just need to ensure everything is normal." She tightly wrapped the top of Alice's arm with a band before tapping with two fingers at Alice's veins.

"But they took my blood in New Zealand."

"I prefer to take my own samples," Dr. Diane said sternly, inserting a needle into the chosen vein. "Also, I recommend establishing a good exercise routine for your mental well-being and overall health. People tend to feel cooped up down here."

"How many seasons have you been the winter-over doctor?" Alice inquired.

"This is my second season. But that's all I'm allowed to divulge; Ryder has forbidden us from giving you interviews. Apologies, my dear."

It was worth a shot.

Alice thanked the doctor and returned to her room, now equipped with everything she needed to start her research. She settled at her tiny desk and opened a spreadsheet on her laptop. She copied the text from the roster image and pasted it into the spreadsheet, alphabetizing her subjects, and got to work.

For several days, she remained secluded in her windowless chamber, venturing out only for sustenance and bathroom breaks. Among the fifty-one scientist winter-overs on the station, comprising sixteen Americans, sixteen Britons, eight Australians, six Chileans, three New Zealanders, and two Japanese, all had undergone exhaustive professional scrutiny, background checks, drug screenings, rigorous medical evaluations, and psychological assessments—requirements that summer scientists were exempt from. These individuals seemed almost superhuman, possessing remarkable intelligence and physical aptitude. Many had previous experience at the South Pole, but mostly in the summer months. Their detailed profiles were easily accessible through blogs, peer-reviewed articles, and college profiles, offering ample material for further investigation with the right digital tools and sleuthing techniques.

It was 2:00 in the morning on her fourth night when Alice finally forwarded all her findings to Max. Though she anxiously awaited confirmation of her email's delivery, it was hindered by the sporadic internet connectivity—a known issue as briefed prior to her arrival.

To occupy her time, she decided to explore the station's corridors, familiarizing herself with her home for the coming months. Having memorized the station's layout, she now wandered out on a firsthand exploration. The station sprawled over 80,000 square feet and stood two stories high, elevated on stilts to mitigate snow accumulation. Its modular design resembled a comb, with four branches extending outward. The early morning hour ensured the hallways were deserted, allowing her solitude as she roamed the upper level, inspecting the movie lounge and weight room. Along the way, she noted the commemorative plaques of previous winter-over groups—a sea of faces.

Alice took a quick right and descended through the 'Beer Can,' the vertical tower adjacent to her living quarters, where she discovered the harsh reality of its unheated interior. It mirrored the bone-chilling temperatures outside, just without the wind, which were currently hovering near minus sixty degrees Fahrenheit. Pausing to catch her breath, she felt the humidity in her lungs nearly crystallize, her exhalations forming visible puffs in the frigid air. Quickening her pace down the stairs, she found refuge in the warmth of the controlled environment on the bottom level through the double-stacked doors.

The first room she encountered was the dry sauna. Alice noticed its placement was on the opposite side of the station from the gym in both direction and elevation. *Inconvenient,* she thought, *but useful information, nonetheless.* Observing additional berthing units nearby and a staircase offering an alternative route to the upper level, she made a mental note to avoid the Beer Can and its freezing air whenever possible, especially when not equipped with her parka.

Passing by the dormant mail room, she arrived at 'Polemart,' the station's store, seldom open yet stocked with essential supplies as listed in her handbook. Right next door, Alice discovered what she deemed the station's best room: the Greenhouse. Stepping inside, she was greeted by twinkling lights suspended from the ceiling, illuminating a space alive with lush green vegetation thriving under UV lights and running on a hydroponic system. Despite only being there for a few days, she already missed the lush greenery and humidity of the California coastline. Alice lingered, breathing in the rich smell of life.

She was interrupted by the arrival of Dr. Diane, clad in gloves and armed with shears. "Ms. Lewis, up so early?" the doctor inquired, getting right to work.

"Insomnia," Alice fibbed, masking her true preoccupation with station-wide reconnaissance in lieu of conducting interviews.

"Perfect timing then. I could use your help. Fill three bags of spinach for the cooks," the doctor instructed.

Gratefully accepting the task, Alice was happy to get some gardening in, reminiscing about her herb garden she kept in the window of her camper van.

"All volunteers work down here in the Greenhouse.

Perhaps you could persuade Ryder to let you join the team," the doctor suggested optimistically.

"I'd like that," Alice agreed.

"I'll speak to him," the doctor promised, departing with her harvest.

Left to resume her self-guided tour, Alice continued on, exploring the laundry room, a cozy and tranquil library, and a goodwill hallway offering items for sharing or taking. Spotting a strand of battery-operated twinkle lights accompanied by a rechargeable battery set, she claimed them, hoping to bring some warmth to her berthing. Continuing her exploration, she ventured into the craft room, music room, and the expansive gym, completing her full circuit of the station. Climbing the nearest staircase, she ascended back to the top level and back to her berthing.

Alice opened her laptop and saw that the email had finally gone through to Max, but there was still no response. She set up her twinkle lights and lay down beneath them. She soon fell soundly asleep, only to be awakened several hours later by the *bing* of an incoming email.

Hi Alice,

Great job on the reconnaissance regarding the current staff. My source reviewed your information and advised that you should focus on the following individuals:

- Dr. Marcus Valen

- Dr. Ethan Carmichael

- Dr. Diane Chen

- Ryder Wilson

They are the only personnel who have been present during the last two winters and are now there for a third winter. If anyone knows what is going on, it will be them.

Please update me once you have more information.

Best regards, Max

Alice sat pensively for a moment. She opened her spreadsheet, highlighted the names, and pulled up their corresponding images she had found online. She took note of Dr. Diane and Ryder, but she was more interested in her two new targets.

Dr. Marcus Valen was an American astrophysicist with a master's degree in Particle Physics. He was a short stocky man in his mid-fifties, with dark brown hair and wire frame glasses. Dr. Ethan Carmichael, in stark contrast, was a young man in his late twenties from Oxford, who ran marathons in his spare time when he wasn't engrossed in his study of Theoretical Physics.

After getting dressed, Alice headed to breakfast. Powdered eggs and spinach were on the menu, and she was eager to try some of the harvest she had helped collect in the early hours of the morning. Choosing a table farthest from the exit, she positioned her back against the wall to observe the other inhabitants as they came and went, while attempting to appear engrossed in her meal. Thankfully, nobody really took any notice of her presence, and to her delight, the IceCube scientists came in and chose to sit at the table closest to Alice.

Although they were speaking in English, Alice couldn't understand a word they were saying.

"Well, would it still work without vacuum-insulated panels? The only way it would stay in its form is if it had low thermal conductivity and could minimize heat transfer," Dr. Marcus Valen spouted off as he took a seat, pushing up his glasses before picking up his fork.

"Well, you wouldn't want a cooling mechanism, but a vapor-compression system is efficient and works well in cold environments. Thermoelectric extractors offer more control but are less efficient," Dr. Ethan Carmichael corrected him in a proper British accent, pushing his flowing blond hair out of his face before starting on his meal. "This is ridiculous; we wouldn't be able to smuggle those types of ingredients over there anyway."

A crackle came from all the radios in the galley, and the room went quiet, awaiting the announcement on the other end. A voice Alice didn't recognize came over the radio. "Marcus or Ethan, come in. You have an alarm."

Everyone in the room went back to breakfast except for the two who were summoned and who immediately engaged in an aggressive game of rock, paper, scissors.

Ethan was victorious and remained seated while Marcus radioed back, advising he was on his way. After he departed, Alice got up and took his seat.

"Hi, I'm Alice." She extended her hand to Ethan who projected a Clark Kent aura, nerdy but had great potential in the looks department with a little primping.

"Good morning, Alice. I'm Ethan. To what do I owe the pleasure of your company?"

"I couldn't help but overhearing your conversation and not understanding a word you said. Would you mind elaborating?"

Ethan laughed. "Oh we were trying to decipher if we could keep ice cream over at the IceCube."

"Ice cream, in Antarctica?" She raised an eyebrow.

"Well, we have it here," he motioned to the little ice cream fridge against the wall, "but we want some over at the other office too."

"Is that where your friend was off to?" She purposely avoided using the doctor's name.

"I'm not supposed to answer your questions. Ryder would have my head." He pointed his fork at Alice, throwing her a flirtatious scowl.

"I guess he got to everyone," she surmised.

"Indeed he did, but if you help him out with some tasks and warm up to him, he may let up on the great 'Journo Embargo of 2024.' If you would excuse me, Alice, I should probably go help Marcus." He nodded to Alice and walked away almost as quickly as he had sat down, returning his unfinished breakfast to the kitchen.

Alice was annoyed. *That was a futile swing and a miss.* But at least she now had her next task. Twice she had been told to get on Ryder's good side, and that was exactly what she planned on doing. She had prepared for such an event and went straight back to her berthing to grab what she needed.

Before long, she was standing in front of the communications room. It was mostly unused in the winter but was where Ryder could usually be found. She knocked on the door, peering through the window to see Ryder turn around in his swivel chair before coming to the door. Alice held up her peace offering to the window: a one-pound bag of Lindt Lindor Chocolate Truffles. Ryder's eyes went wide.

"I wouldn't be wavin' that around. That's as good as gold down here," he said after ensuring the hallway was clear.

"I know, I did my research. It's the only thing you can eat while outside, right?"

"Yeah, and I once watched a scientist barter away three days of snow clearin' duty for five pieces of that chocolate." Ryder snatched at the bag, but Alice pulled it behind her back.

"I want an exchange," Alice bargained.

Ryder's face went flat with annoyance. "What do ya want?"

"I want to work in the Greenhouse."

"It's voluntary, do what ya please."

"I also want a tour of the legendary ice tunnels, and I want to interview the IceCube scientists." She took a deep breath, holding it in anticipation of his response.

"Bloody never," he replied, reaching around Alice's back to snag the chocolate, but she refused to let go. He pulled her in close and looked down on her, their noses almost touching. He sniffed. "Seems as if you have already partaken in eating some of these chocolates."

Alice's face turned bright red, both from embarrassment and the realization that she found Ryder attractive. Startled, she let go of the bag. Ryder pursed his lips and winked before slamming the door on Alice, nearly missing her nose. Again.

"Asshole," she whispered, turning around and walking away.

'*Failure is a state of mind*,' she thought, quoting John Steinbeck. Walking down the long corridor to the other side of the station, she once again passed the images of the previous winter- over groups. Pausing to take a closer look, she noticed something she hadn't seen the night before. All four of the previous winter overs on her list were standing together, and next to them in the photo from last season was the man who had handed her the barf bag during their descent to the station. His piercing ice-blue eyes were framed by jet-black hair and a notably weak jawline. Alice couldn't recall seeing him since her arrival, but now she decided to figure out where he might be hiding. She took out her phone, zoomed in on the mystery man, and took a picture.

A simple reverse image search yielded only two images of the man online, neither providing valuable information, not even a name. He was some sort of enigma. The first image was identical to the one on the wall in the corridor, and the second image was from a blog of a scientist who had been at the station the previous season. The mystery man appeared in a group of scientists celebrating Easter in the mess hall, all wearing festive bunny ears, with no other identifying details.

Alice decided to investigate the old-fashioned way, starting in the weight room. There, she found two men on treadmills watching one of the Harry Potter movies as they walked, completely transfixed on the screen. She didn't stay long enough to find out if their nerd trance could be broken and headed downstairs to the gymnasium. Poking her head into the largest room on the station, she saw a morning yoga class being led by Dr. Diane. In unison, the group turned and noticed Alice standing in the doorway. She slipped out before they asked her to join and continued her search through the lower level, working her way through the relatively quiet corridor except for a few people exiting their berthings to start the day. Alice made it all the way to the cold doors leading to the double doors that would take her up the Beer Can, which she didn't dare brave again without a coat and proper gear.

Feeling somewhat defeated after having scoured the majority of the public space in the station without spotting her target, she turned around to head back to her berthing to reformulate her plan. As if on cue, the dry sauna door opened slowly and the mystery man stepped out.

She had to act quickly. "Hi there!" she called, closing the distance between them so fast that when he turned around, she nearly bumped into him. Stepping back, she said the first thing that came to her mind. "Thank you for giving me the barf bag on the plane last week. I didn't catch your name."

Her extended hand hovered as he observed her obtrusive approach for a long beat. "That's because I did not tell you my name," he said in a staccato cadence, his hand then meeting hers in a firm grasp. Almost instantly Alice let go; his hand was ice cold.

There was a long pause before he responded with an emotionless glare. "Charles Carroll."

Alice cradled her hand. "I'm Alice." Smiling politely, she was filled with unease. She knew full well there was no Charles Carroll on the station, having combed the roster until her eyes nearly bled over the previous days, and there was no good reason that the man's hands should be so cold coming out of the sauna.

Curiously, he didn't explain his post at the station. Instead, he awkwardly attempted to smile, put on his big red snow jacket that had been hanging outside the sauna, and headed into the Beer Can without saying another word.

Alice wasn't about to follow him into the ice tube of death unprepared. She ran back down the hall, up the stairs, and waited at the top, out of breath, her lungs begging for air, the 9,300-foot altitude exhibiting its wrath. She waited patiently for Charles to come through the double doors, casually waving as someone walked by her, pity filling their eyes at her state of exhaustion.

But he never showed.

Alice quickly went back to her berthing, put on multiple layers, her mittens, a thick beanie, and her issued red parka before she headed back to the Beer Can. A rush of cold air hit her, taking her breath away as she entered. There was no sign of Charles as she cautiously headed down the stairs.

Upon reaching the bottom where she would have turned to go through the doors to the lower level of the station, she instead shone her flashlight around a corner where the stairs continued down even further. She followed them down several more flights, finally landing at the bottom and facing a long hallway with a putrid yellow floor. The walls and ceiling were lined with pipes, likely holding electrical wiring and other infrastructural necessities. According to Alice's research, she was in what was referred to as the 'Arches,' where the station's storage facilities resided. This is where the food, building materials, fuel supplies, water resources, and septic systems were kept. The tunnel ran the length of the station with several offshoots.

The hum of the station's lifeblood filled her ears, accompanied by the thud of her own anxious heartbeat. Alice treaded slowly, walking as quietly as she could along the metal grates. Signs labeled the different facility purposes along the way, but there was still no sign of Charles Carroll anywhere. Then she heard a muted *thunk* from one of the corridors. No markings or signs indicated what might be down there. Taking a deep breath, she whispered to herself, "Oh Alice, 'we're all mad here'." And she headed down the rabbit hole.

After ducking under a large pipe, Alice made her way along the metal grate floor. The walls transitioned from lined metal pipes to snow and ice, and the temperature was even colder than it had been above. Her cheeks ached from the chill. Most of the pipes had dispersed and closed off, but two large pipes and attached lighting continued down the hallway. The metal grates of the floor were soon covered by snow and ice, and everything around her turned white except for the two remaining pipes, indicating the tunnel's original purpose. The snowy floor squeaked and crunched under her feet with every step, reminding her she had forgotten her issued crampons. Several footprints lined the path, but there was no telling if they belonged to the man she pursued.

Stopping, she held her breath and noticed the complete silence around her. The snow and ice muted all sounds, and there was no sign of anyone else nearby, so she continued on. She could only speculate about her position in these legendary ice tunnels.

Alice came across a carved-out cove. She'd read that the station's residents would come down here to leave memorials and tidbits of history over the years. This was why she had originally asked Ryder for a tour of the ice tunnels—mostly for her own entertainment and curiosity. But now, she was down here without permission and knew she couldn't simply peruse. An artifact caught her eye; it was a tub of vanilla ice cream labeled "THE LAST TUB OF VANILLA ICE CREAM WINTER 2012." Alice laughed, wondering if Marcus and Ethan knew about this.

Continuing on, she passed through a rudimentary wooden door that may have been locked but was now splintered and open. She now was crossing a threshold where she knew she was out of bounds, and apparently she wasn't the first to cross this line today. On the other side was more tunnel, with more shrines of eclectic arti-facts. Every few feet, there were peculiar memorials, including ice sculptures, cakes, puppets, an electric chainsaw, and even a whole sturgeon. Alice didn't allow herself to get distracted. Her eyelashes were starting to develop ice crystals, which she attempted to wipe away to no avail. She was very cold and unsure of how much more exposure she could take.

Not much further along the tunnel there was a split; one of the large pipes took a hard right, and Alice instinctively decided to follow it. Another twenty yards down, the ceiling started to slope where beautiful ice crystals formed. The pipes also sloped down, and Alice had to bend down low to continue. The path stopped at a slightly ajar small wooden door, barely two and a half feet high. Alice got down on her stomach and crawled through. On the other side of the door, the tunnel remained cramped for several feet until it opened up, overlooking a vast chasm filled with water and rising steam. A catwalk crossed the spherical ice cave, supported by metal columns angled into the ice on either side. Icicles formed along the railings of the catwalk, which led to a metal door on the other side of the void—this door was large enough for a person to walk through.

Alice surmised this was where the station's fresh water was sourced. The process involved pumping warm water into the ice, which was then sucked back out through the system, with the Antarctic ice providing an endless supply of life to the residents above.

Positioning herself in the center of the walkway, the steam rose around Alice as she stood, taking in the other-worldly view. Suddenly, she heard voices coming from the tunnel she had just exited. Two men were arguing as they made their way through the crawl space. Alice ran across to the larger door and sighed in relief when it easily opened. On the other side, a bare ice tunnel stretched endlessly into an arch, with no lighting or electrical wires in sight. She pulled the metal door closed, turned on her flashlight, and ran as quickly as she could without risking a fall, following the tunnel until the arch concealed the view of the door behind her. Then she turned off her light.

"We should have brought Ryder into the fold last year. He is working against the objective by not letting the journalist do her job." Alice recognized the voice coming through the door. It was Marcus, the older IceCube scientist. His voice projected just far enough to be heard along the sound-absorbent walls.

Keeping her flashlight off, she crept along the tunnel wall as quietly as she could, trailing her hand along the icy curve of the tunnel. Wanting to create space and stay ahead as they approached, she took increasingly large steps, groping in the dark until her hand hit air.

The tunnel wall made a hard right angle. Putting her hands out in front of her, she touched some kind of solid structure. It was a metal ladder. Feeling it was her best option to avoid being seen by the two men, she began to climb.

Going up ten rungs, she felt the walls closing in, her jacket scratching against the sides. The space above was tightly enclosed, and instead of climbing any higher, she pulled her legs up as far as she could while the men's voices drew closer.

"It would be easier to just implant him like we did last year at the end of the season. We have it all planned out."

"It's too early in the season to start that, Marcus. We haven't even positioned the IceCube for transport, and people would notice, specifically that woman. I can't risk him malfunctioning like some of the others." Alice recognized Ethan's British accent.

Their flashlights lit the tunnel below. Alice held her breath, silently praying they didn't look up at the ladder as they passed.

"This is ridiculous. We should have never agreed to bring a reporter down here in the first place, let alone one we hadn't cleared," Ethan continued as they both passed below Alice. "Have you spoken with the holdover who came back yet?"

"No, he is keeping out of sight as ordered. I couldn't alter the manifest to put Brant's name on there, and I have no clue how he managed to get on the plane. But I hope he enjoyed his romp around our world. This will be the first time anyone ever goes back, but there is obviously something very wrong." Marcus's voice faded into the snow-lined walls as he moved further down the tunnel.

Alice's blood ran cold—and not because of the negative extremely low air temperature. She had just stumbled upon the most important story in history. She clung to the ladder until her arms ached, waiting until the men were out of earshot before turning her flashlight back on. Looking up the ladder, which extended many more feet higher, presumably to an escape hatch above, she realized she was likely halfway to the IceCube observatory if she was recalling the station's layout correctly.

Alice considered whether to follow the scientists or go back and warn Ryder—a tough decision she didn't take lightly. Finally, she crawled down the ladder and slowly headed back down the curved hallway towards the water processing room. Taking her time to ensure nobody was coming from ahead or behind, she made her way through the metal door, across the catwalk, and got down on her knees as the steam swept up around her. Reaching for the wooden door to push it forward, her mitten met no resistance—the door was being pulled open by Ryder.

"What the bloody hell are you doing down here?"

he snarled, moving forward and pushing her back into the spherical chamber.

Coming to her feet, Alice brushed off excess snow from her knees. "I was following a lead."

"The hell ya were, ya nosy nelly. Do you know how dangerous it is down here?"

Alice almost choked on the irony. "We've got to get you out of here, Ryder. Turn around and let's go. You are the one who is in danger. There are bigger things happening here than a safety violation."

"Hell naur. Not until ya explain how ya found yer way down here."

They stood in a stalemate on the catwalk. Then the metal door leading to the dark ice tunnel swung open.

The man with the ice blue eyes stood there, steam rising at his feet.

"What the hell are ya doing here, Dr. Brant?" Ryder asked.

The man's eyes swept to Alice, waiting for her response; the expression on his face remained void of any emotion.

"Dr. Brant? Are you sure it's not Charles Carroll?" Alice challenged, looking between the two men.

"Charles? Who's that?" Ryder looked at the man, perplexed by Alice's challenge. "That's who he introduced himself as," Alice said, gesturing to the stranger.

"There isn't anyone on this station by either name, but the bloke I'm lookin' at was here last season, and his name is Dr. Brant. But he most certainly isn't supposed to be here this year. So who the hell are you?"

The man charged full speed and lunged at Alice and Ryder. Ryder stepped in front of Alice, taking the initial blow. The metal lattice beneath their feet shuddered as the two men slammed into the suspended walkway. The man mechanically maneuvered his leg to hook Ryder's, pulling his body into the top position. Despite his best efforts, Ryder's mitten-covered hands failed to grasp the man above him. His opponent's reach was much longer, and he easily slipped his bare hands around Ryder's neck.

Alice watched in terror as Ryder's face drained. She flung off her mittens and gripped one of the icicles dangling from the edge of the walkway. Pulling back with all her strength she broke off a two-foot spear of ice. She ran at the man and plunged the icicle into the base of his neck. He immediately went limp on top of Ryder.

Alice removed the icicle, leaving a gaping hole that oozed a thick black liquid from the edges of the wound. The same substance that now stained Alice's hands was definitely not blood. It was much warmer than blood and caused the impromptu weapon to quickly dissolve in her palms. Alice dropped the remaining ice and watched it shatter into multiple dark chunks at her feet.

She went to pull the body off Ryder, but it was much heavier than she had anticipated, and she fell backward as she yanked the body free. With the momentum it tumbled off the platform into the water below. Ryder sat up, gasping for air and getting his feet beneath him. "Thank you," he said, outstretching his hand to Alice. "Let's get out of here."

"No, Dr. Valen and Dr. Carmichael are responsible for what just happened. They know what's going on. I have to find out the truth and what that thing is."

Alice studied the black liquid on her hands and wiped as much off as she could before putting her mittens back on. She turned around and headed towards the ice tunnel where Marcus and Ethan had gone. Before she went through the metal door, she turned back to Ryder who was staring at her in disbelief.

"Are you coming?"

He looked up as if asking for guidance from a higher power and then looked back at Alice. "I can't stop ya, can I?"

She shook her head. "Nope."

The two stealthily made their way along the curve of the ice tunnel.

"Where does this lead?" Alice asked, shining her light ahead.

Ryder's voice was raspy from the attack, and he hoarsely whispered his response. "It's the tunnel to the IceCube and other outbuildings, depending on which direction ya take. The scientists are only supposed to use it in an emergency, when the weather is too bad to cross by foot durin' the dark months."

They continued down the passage and passed Alice's previous hiding place. Ryder shined his flashlight up the ladder. "This time of year, the escape hatches are a dead end because we don't clear them from the inside. It's just too cold. What are we going to do once we get to the end? Should we go back for more icicles?" Ryder asked tauntingly after a few more minutes of walking.

"Too soon," Alice replied sternly, still shaking from the shock of killing a man, or whatever it was, with her own hands.

There were several offshoots, but Ryder directed Alice to remain along the main tunnel. It wasn't long until they arrived at another metal door. Ryder pulled out keys to unlock it, opening it with a loud creak. The automatic lights turned on, leading to a stairwell to take them up and out of the ice tunnel.

"Where is the telescope?" Alice asked, expecting to see some sort of geometric dome.

"It's under the ice. We've actually been walking over the sensors since the edge of the water generator. It's a kilometer long, and the sensors go down 1.5 miles to the bedrock. The idea is that it can detect neutrinos that travel hundreds of millions, even billions, of miles from space for scientists to study."

"So the sensors are underneath us now?"

"Yup."

Alice suddenly felt very small as they climbed their way up into the laboratory. Entering through double doors, the temperature warmed up significantly in the main room, which was filled with computers and server equipment twinkling in the dark. The double doors behind them slammed shut, drawing out the occupants of the corner office.

Marcus and Ethan emerged from the office and strode towards Alice and Ryder.

"They aren't going to be happy." Ethan shook his head.

"Exactly who is 'they'? Would it be whoever sent the bloke to off me?" Ryder spared no time cutting to the chase, posturing for a fistfight.

"Let's all just calm down," Marcus said in a hushed tone.

"Calm down? Really? I heard everything you said in the tunnel." Alice turned to explain to Ryder, "They know everything. Including why the personnel have been 'malfunctioning' after they returned home for the summer."

"How did you know about that, Alice?" Ryder looked at her in surprise.

Marcus sat down in an empty chair and took off his glasses to clean them, while Ethan walked over to the wall and turned on the lights. Marcus reached for a cabinet and grabbed a bottle of brown liquor, unscrewing the cap. "Well, where did Brant go? How did you sneak past him?" he asked, taking a sip straight from the bottle.

"I killed him," Alice whispered.

Marcus spit out his drink.

"Oh they aren't going to like that," Ethan said quietly.

"Who the bloody hell is 'they'?" Ryder demanded.

Marcus stood up and grabbed Alice by her jacket. "Where is the body?"

She shoved him off before Ryder could come to her rescue. "I pushed it into the water generator." Her voice cracked, forcing out the words.

"You let her do that?" Marcus looked wide eyed at Ryder.

"It wasn't intentional mate." After a few long moments of silence, a crackle over the radio called for Ryder. "Go ahead."

"An alarm went off; the water generator is malfunctioning," a concerned voice advised through the small handheld speaker.

"Shut it down. Advise the crew we are under emergency water rations."

"The water supply is the least of your problems once they realize that you killed their holdover." Marcus looked at the ground, seemingly spiraling into some kind of depression.

"Last chance. Someone, anyone, answer me. Who is 'they'?" Ryder demanded once again.

The scientists looked at each other.

Alice, deep down, already knew. "I think 'they'"—Alice air-quoted—"are not from this Earth."

"Ding, ding, ding... She's a smart girl." Marcus took another long gulp from the bottle, clearly showing the beginning signs of intoxication.

"Spill it. Tell us everything," Alice pleaded, looking at Ethan.

Heaving a deep breath into his lungs, Ethan responded while looking at his colleague with disappointment. "When the telescope was built in 2010, it took them no longer than forty-five minutes to reach out to us once it was powered up. Their technology is exceptional, and their ability to defy all the laws of physics still baffles us to this day. They made it here roughly two seasons ago."

Alice furrowed her brow. "How could they communicate instantly if it took them twelve years to get here?"

"We haven't figured that out yet. We also haven't figured out how they pair with our bodies and why most aren't working but some are. What we do know is they can't perfectly pair with everyone. Hence the issues that you apparently already know about, Ms. Lewis." Ethan took a deep breath and dove into further detail. "Dr. Brant was the first one that came back who they were going to attempt to separate after being embodied for such a long period of time."

"How do ya know that it would've worked?" Ryder challenged him.

"Because we have assisted in separating people after short periods of time. Specifically on you, you overgrown kangaroo," Marcus quipped in between swigs.

"You have got to be bloody kiddin' me. You IceCube blokes have been hiding this for over a decade and are allowing aliens to run amok on Earth?" Ryder's voice trailed off, not believing what he was saying. "Including inside me!" He pawed at himself, wiping away an invisible muck from his arms and hands.

"Yes, one small misstep for man, and one giant disastrous end for all mankind." Marcus finished off the bottle of liquor. "But it will all be for the better someday."

"It's really not that bad." Ethan tried to explain. "In your case, Ryder, we knew you wouldn't agree, so when you are embodied you have no memory. In my case it's completely symbiotic and I quite enjoy it."

The entire room started to flash red before either Alice or Ryder could respond. Ethan ran into the control room, the rest of them following. He sat down in front of a black screen and started typing commands in Linux. A matrix screen of thousands of characters not of this world responded.

"Now what?" Alice asked.

"We don't know, but killing one of them isn't something we've encountered; it seems like they know." He typed in some commands, and the gibberish turned to English in front of their eyes.

This woman is compatible. She will do.

"Oh thank God." Marcus sighed with relief.

Ethan stood up, pushed back his chair, and put Ryder into a choke hold.

Alice had no time to react. Marcus shattered his empty liquor bottle over her head, knocking her unconscious.

* * *

Alice awoke, staring into darkness. Her head pulsed with a pressure she had never felt before, and she could hear her own heartbeat picking up speed. It was still very cold, but she didn't think she was on the ice. In fact, she wasn't even laying down at all. It felt more like she was being cradled; her hands and feet were shackled, not allowing her to move.

"She's awake." A familiar woman's voice filled the room. Then a faint blue light illuminated the space just enough for Alice to see she was indeed in a chair, and next to her was Ryder, still unconscious.

"Why?" Alice asked. "Why would you do this?"

"We may as well tell her," Ethan's voice interjected. "She is going to know soon enough."

"Fine. Hopefully, it will make the transition go more smoothly. Alice, you have been deemed compatible to be a host."

Alice recognized the voice; it was Dr. Diane. *She*

must have lied about the purpose of the blood draw. She pulled against the restraints at her wrists. "Let me go!"

"We can't do that. We need you to fulfill a very important role." Ethan's voice echoed within the chamber. "The journalist who had originally been slotted for your spot down here was perfect, but thankfully you will do as well. We humans are so easily influenced these days, and they have asked us to assist in the infiltration of the media next. They have the scientific world under control, but now they need to gain the control of the mass population."

There was silence for a few moments. Alice looked over at Ryder who was still out cold. He looked peaceful. *At least he won't feel anything.*

"Alice, things are going to get dark, and then the symbiosis will be complete. Don't fight it. If anything, help them out and your life will be much more comfortable and mostly normal," Ethan directed.

A loud hum filled the room and the blue light became brighter. "What happens if I fight it?" she screamed over the noise.

"Then you won't be there to witness history."

"Alice..." Ryder grumbled over the hum as he began to wake up.

She caught his glance, and there was no fear or anger reflected in his eyes, only tranquility. *'He looked at her the way all women want to be looked at by a man,'* Alice thought to herself, a quote from *The Great Gatsby.*

Then the bright light and hum dulled all of her senses, and everything went black.

* * *

The newsroom of the top rated cable news network in the country was on the bottom floor of one of the most prestigious buildings in New York City. The backdrop of the news desk looked out onto a square where busy New Yorkers could be seen going to work or school, or tourists out early to see the sights. None of them were aware the world was about to change forever.

Alice had been the main host of the morning program for nearly three weeks now. She was sitting in her dressing room, the make-up artist putting on the finishing touches to ensure she was camera-ready. "Three minutes, Alice, break a leg." The make-up artist shut the door behind her, leaving the anchor to her thoughts before she went on air.

Do you think they will like us? asked the voice inside her head, the voice that had not been her own for three years.

Looking deep into the mirror she responded, "I hope so. But at this point they don't have a choice, do they?"

No, not particularly. Do remember that if this goes well, Ryder can come to New York permanently.

"Yes, I know. You have reminded me of that from day one." Alice struggled to verbalize her criticism.

Oh, don't be so sassy, Alice. We gave you your dream to be a top investigative reporter.

Alice got up and headed down the hallway to the studio. She stepped up onto the stage and took her position behind the big plexiglass desk. The teleprompter counted down from thirty seconds. But there were no words cued for her to read after that, not today. The floor producer counted down with his fingers three, two, one...

"Good morning, everyone, and thank you all for joining me at this early hour. While you may have expected to hear the latest updates in politics and world news, today I want to discuss something profoundly important.

"We inhabit an astonishing planet, Earth, which supports life in countless unique and sometimes inexplicable forms. From tiny single-celled organisms to whales longer than three school buses, our world is a tapestry of incredible beauty and diversity. From lush rainforests to vast arid deserts, every sunrise and sunset, every blooming flower and flowing river, speaks to the wonder of our home. These are constant reminders that we are part of something much greater than ourselves.

"What truly makes Earth extraordinary is humanity. We possess the capacity for love, compassion, creativity, and innovation, giving us a unique ability to shape our world. Our interconnectedness binds us, and our shared experiences and dreams unite us. In moments of joy and sorrow, triumph and challenge, we come together, proving time and again the strength of the human spirit.

"In the hustle and bustle of our daily lives, it's easy to lose sight of this larger picture. We get caught up in routines, worries, and the endless stream of noise. But it's essential to pause occasionally and reflect, to appreciate the incredible world we live in and the people who make it so special.

"Let's remember that our actions, no matter how small, have a ripple effect. A smile, a kind word, a helping hand—they all contribute to making our world a better place. Let's cherish our planet and each other, for we are all part of this beautiful mosaic of life.

"Please take a moment to absorb what I've said."

Alice and her companion speaking through her paused...

"Because today, I am here to reveal that we are not alone in this universe, and it's time to share Earth with a species who is just as special as our own."

Kara Smith, a career intelligence analyst and Air Force OIF/OEF Veteran, has worked with the NSA, AFOSI, FBI, and law enforcement nationwide. Outside her work, she's a mother, outdoor enthusiast, cinephilia, travel addict, and animal lover. Too keep up with Kara's writing endeavors check out https://karasmithbooks.com

Good for the Game

Ursula Vogt

arlo stood on the private dock watching the lazy slap of waves against the *Love Thy Neighbor*. It was a gorgeous 250-foot yacht anchored half a mile off the Miami coast. On any other day, the rhythm could have lulled her for hours. There seemed to be a symbiotic relationship, as if the image wouldn't be complete without both the sparkling water and the sway of the ship on its surface. Pictures online didn't do it justice. It was a regal piece of art, its sleek lines floating in the spotlight of the Florida rays. For just a moment she felt guilty, as if it were just another undeserving victim.

But it wasn't art, she reminded herself. It was a trophy.

A staff guard reached in with a security wand, interrupting her thoughts as he began herding all ten of them away from the water's edge and underneath the blue registration tent. Inside, four long folding tables lined the back wall where his partner waited, hands on hips. They both looked like someone washed FBI agents in bleach. White hair, high and tight...white shirts...white deck shoes...Cartier platinum sunglasses. The only splash of color was their heavy tans.

She looked down at the wand paused an inch from her chest as the guard perved for just a few seconds longer than necessary. Marlo slid her own sunglasses down and stared at him like a junior high teacher assessing his future in the world. They stared at each other, or at least she thought they did because, honestly, with the mirrored shades, it felt like she was looking at some soulless robot until he grinned and dropped the wand.

"Move your bags to the table. Everything will be searched," he bellowed to the entire group, even though he continued staring at Marlo. "Cell phones are not allowed on board, so turn them off, now." He fired off the security riff so close to her face she could probably guess what brand of gum he chewed. "Seal them in a plastic zip-top bag, and then place them in the bin." He pointed to his bleached-out security twin who put empty TSA-style bins on the tables and waited in a military At Ease stance. They all moved forward and began filling them with their travel gear.

His orders lacked color, too. Flat and heavy with

implication, they left no room for discussion, which Marlo understood was the point. Cy had prepped her well. He had also given her a burner and told her under no circumstances was she to bring her personal phone, even in the car. Especially in the car. It wasn't until much later she learned that he knew security would search everyone's vehicles as soon as they left the dock.

So, after her final conversation with Cy in the parking lot, the one where they each had the option to either walk away, or go forward with the plan, Marlo had pulled the SIM card from the burner and let it slip into the water as she walked onto the dock. The decision came with significant risk. They were gambling with the lives of everyone on board.

Now, with the gutted burner bagged and tagged, the mission was officially a go, and she was on her own.

First on the list: Pass the security check.

Bleach twin number two stepped up to the table, took a deep breath and snapped his latex gloves at the wrist before diving into her bin. He dumped the contents of her bag and smoothed his gloved hands over the lining and zipper. Next, he emptied her wallet, checked her lipstick, took the pepper spray off her keychain, broke it down into three pieces that were all tossed in a trash bin, and finished by running a wand over the contents. When nothing alerted, he shoved the bin aside without returning the contents to her bag.

"Is this your first time on board?" A bouncy blonde with an Aussie accent landed her heavy Gucci beach bag in the bin next to hers. Her uniform was a bit different from Marlo's all black, Amy Winehouse-style skirt and tank. A tight crimson t-shirt, white shorts, white tennis shoes, baseball hat with a ponytail out the back, a fresh manicure that matched her shirt, gold hoop earrings, and sunglasses. That seemed to be the uniform for all nine of the others. "I'm Ivy. I tend bar for the Howards' big weekend every year." She gave Marlo a smile that clearly cost her thousands and started unloading her bag, too. Marlo checked her very short French white manicure and adjusted the clip holding a mountain of hair in place. So, this was Florida style, she thought.

Ivy Parker. Twenty-two. five-foot, three-inches. Single. Moved up from Rawlinna, Australia, the largest sheep station in the world. Attended bartending school in Miami, presumably because, well, that was a shit-ton of sheep, and she was probably ready for the human experience. Works exclusively for private floating casinos up and down the coast. Employed by the Howards for the last three out of five trips.

Cy had drilled Marlo on the background of every person on board, except the bleach twins. They were a bit sketchy, but as long as she assumed they were excellent at their jobs, the only crucial data to know was that she was better. At least she had to be for the next two days.

"Let's have that case up here, too." Twin number two interrupted and pointed at the rolling case Marlo had bought on Amazon to house her gear. She heaved it up on the table, and he waved the scanner over the edges. The meter screamed and the guard's nostrils flared like a bull with a target. "Open it," he demanded, hands back on hips and legs spread wide.

"Ah, it's just the chips," Marlo told him with an embarrassed grin as she opened the case. Everyone was staring at them. "Poker chips have an RFDI strip in them now. Well, the good ones do, anyway." *A five-second pause, just like they'd practiced...* "It's a security thing. But you knew that, sorry. I should have declared them when I rolled up...my mistake."

Cy had explained that security would go crazy when her bag alerted, and she would be on their radar for the rest of the cruise if she didn't give him an out and make him look good. After all, she was the only new crew member added to the roster on this trip. So, she flashed her own expensive smile and gave him a wink. *You've got this*, it said. *Everyone here knows you recognize the difference between the boss's poker chips and a security threat. You're looking good, though, doing your thing, and keeping them safe. Thumbs up!*

That's the optics everyone around them saw.

Ivy froze at Marlo's side, waiting to see how twin

number two would respond. It was hard to tell if she was amused or frightened, but there was a slight hint of vicarious enjoyment around the edges that Marlo approved of.

She spotted her chance to redirect, as Cy put it, and take the next step. "Hi, Ivy. My friends call me Vegas. I'm the dealer for this trip," she said, as she called the bleach twin's bluff and reclaimed her gear bag without asking permission. "You just keep those drinks comin' and between the two of us, we'll make this the best damn poker run the boss has ever launched." Ivy brought up a fist. *Okay, they were going to fist bump.* She could play along. And there was number two checked off her list: Make an ally as soon as possible.

Twenty minutes later, the entire staff had been checked, and the bags were loaded. They boarded the tender, a twenty-eight-foot cigar boat built for speed, and ferried out to the *Love Thy Neighbor*. Marlo had been a professional Vegas dealer for the last twenty years, so keeping her opinions off her face as they bounced along the water was her default setting. But for the first of many times to come that weekend, she was grateful the person she'd buddied up to was the bartender.

It didn't take long to reach the ship where Ivy offered to give her a quick tour and show her to her cabin. Usually the crew shared bunk rooms, but as the dealer, Marlo had negotiated her own room telling the captain that she needed to ensure the security of the cards and chips. And she couldn't do that, sharing a cabin. He'd argued that the other dealers had never needed that consideration, but Marlo pointed out that the Howards had never hired a pro before this cruise.

As soon as she was alone, she checked the room for bugs and cameras the way Cy had taught her. Cy was her ride-or-die for anything tech related. He claimed to be a white hat, but Marlo wasn't sure any hacker was a complete angel. But for this weekend to succeed, she needed him to be a bit of both.

Feeling fairly certain her cabin was clean, she unpacked everything into the cabin safe. Not that she was under any illusion that security wouldn't check it at some point, but she wanted to prove the pretense. And she wanted to make them work for it.

According to Cy's research, and confirmed by Ivy, it would take about three hours for the crew to ready the ship and the guests to arrive. After that, they would set sail for their "cruise to nowhere" about fifteen miles out to international waters where gambling for money was legal. That gave her time to walk around and find out more about her hosts.

Lea Frakes-Howard. Forty-two. Five-food, seven inches. A southern beauty who graduated Summa cum laude with a degree in International Finance. Mother to Candice, aged seventeen. Married to Reb Howard and part owner of their company, LTN Ministries.

Reb Howard. Fifty-six. Six-foot, four inches. A midwestern farm boy who didn't care what anyone thought about trophy wives. Born and raised in Ohio. A self-made American success story. Proud father, husband, and front man for a sharing ministry that sold private health insurance to the like-minded faithful dedicated to taking care of each other in times of crisis.

Marlo knew better. She leaned over the teak rail and watched the parade of guests arriving below, trying to imagine her mom being welcomed aboard with a hug from Lea the way the other women were. This. This is what her mom had deserved. Beautiful scenery, sparkling water, and a glass of champagne on a carefree summer afternoon. Instead, Bev had spent her summer trying to survive chemo and shuffling medical bills. She had been so scared when she got her cancer diagnosis just over a year ago, and even though she had a poker face, too, the fear showed. Marlo still teared up remembering her mother's shaking hands when they took a break and met in the casino's burger joint. She explained it as if it was just a minor complication in life, and it would all be fine after a few treatments. Instead, it was the beginning of a nightmare her mom didn't deserve.

"Hey, Vegas!" Ivy was waving a glass of something tropical from across the deck. "Come test my new drink. I make a signature cocktail for every cruise." Ivy met her halfway across the plush carpet, balancing something ethereal blue with bright red cherries and a paper umbrella. "This one is for the ladies. I call it, *The Tempted Angel.*" Marlo took a sip. Not bad. Clearly made with the expensive stuff, not the cheap brands that usually go into Long Island Iced Tea and not as sweet as Sex on the Beach. She gave Ivy a thumbs up. "It's a winner." She took another sip to encourage Ivy, but she was a Macallan girl, all the way.

She slipped back to the rail holding her drink but looking for somewhere to discreetly ditch it. The sun was already dipping low to the horizon, and she needed to keep a clear head tonight. Twin One came up the stairs next to her and stopped. "Vegas, the crew does not drink during the cruise. You should know that." He reached out and took the drink and marched back to the bar. Problem solved. She glanced back at Ivy who mouthed an apology, and she laughed.

It was time to go over the agenda for the first night. Everyone would come aboard and get settled, followed by a seafood buffet dinner. The women would retire to the mid-deck of the ship where there was a massive circular white leather couch with a fire pit in the middle —all a discreet distance from the bar. The men would head to the forward deck where Marlo would be waiting behind a professional game table. It all sounded like an ideal way to host a shareholders meeting of the faithful. Marlo smiled pleasantly at the guests who looked up and saw her above.

She pulled a copy of the letter from her pocket and read it again. Her thoughts went back to Bev. She was the entire reason for booking this poker cruise. Her mom was a legend in Las Vegas and Marlo had learned everything watching her. When Bev came into the casino for a visit now, it was like a family reunion. She collected hugs from staff in the little souvenir shops, the lady who ran the coffee kiosk, hotel check-in clerks, and even the pit boss. They loved her there and the news of her illness was a blow.

The thing that gave Bev comfort was that she had invested in a private health insurance group that believed in helping family—their family of subscribers who pooled their money and took care of each other. But she never expected to be the one who needed the help. She was the person everyone went to for a shoulder to cry on, a meal when they hit a rough patch, and sure, even the occasional ride to rehab if that's what they needed. It was in her DNA to be part of making the world around her a better place, so when she heard about LTN's Share Ministry's health plan, it was a no-brainer. The president of the company, Reb Howard, had personally called to welcome her after her application had been accepted, and that personal touch sealed the deal for Bev. She'd found a company with their priorities straight. But something about it never rang true for Marlo.

Bev was almost done with her second chemo treatment when the hospital informed her that her insurance company was refusing to pay, saying her policy had been cancelled. It took several phone calls, but a week later, a document arrived saying that Bev had been dropped for violating the morality clause. It had come to their attention that Bev's previous employment prior to her retirement had been in the gambling industry. And while they wished her well on her journey back to health, they felt it was important to maintain their family values and standards. Unfortunately, gambling was on the list of occupations that didn't reflect their core beliefs.

Our thoughts and prayers go with you.

Marlo reread that line and waved when Lea Howard looked up and motioned around her that the others needed more champagne. "Ivy. I think they need another bottle of champagne below."

"On it. Thanks!" Ivy went down the stairs holding two freshly chilled bottles. "You're going to work out great around here," she whispered over her shoulder on the way past.

The first night went without a hitch. It was a calm night at sea, and Marlo set up on the open-air deck with tiki torches in a semi-circle, lighting her from behind. The players would look out over the Florida night sky, filled with stars. She'd changed into her black pants, white shirt, and black vest, the professional uniform of all dealers, and tamed her hair into a sleek French twist. She brought out her signature scarlet lipstick for the final touch. Now that dinner was over, it was time for Marlo to take center stage.

It was always interesting getting to know the players, and these six men were no exception. It took a bit of time for them to get comfortable. She'd collected all the credit card numbers and authorized each for the obscene buy-in amount. The twins had fallen back into the shadows, because let's face it, no one wants to be reminded that they need security when they're on a fun weekend out of the spotlight. They all teased about how much they needed a chance to just let it all hang out, and the annual LTN Ministries Share Holders Meeting was the perfect solution. No prying eyes. No reporters. No cell phones allowed except in an emergency. No cameras.

She and Ivy worked as a great team, too. Marlo would glance at Ivy and then at a player. A minute later, a fresh drink appeared on the table. If Marlo didn't know what was going on behind the scenes, she would have enjoyed it as much as the guests.

They decided to call it an early night so they could be fresh for the next day and moved into the conversation pit with the ladies. On the way out, Reb's best friend, Travis, walked around the table and slipped her a purple chip along with a pat on the butt. A thousand dollars. She smiled as if it was their little secret. She noticed Ivy watching them over her tray as she served the conversation pit.

Marlo shut down the table and retired the deck without cleaning them. She slipped them all into a plastic bag and stowed them away. Normally after a private game, she discarded the cards so there was no sign of wear and it eliminated the potential of marked cards, although she doubted this group had the first idea of how to do that.

She was officially off the clock. After checking for any sign of the bleach twins, she rolled her bag past the deep golden platter of iced beer sitting like hors d'oeuvres on the bar and grabbed one on the way to her cabin. What were they going to do, fire her?

Marlo walked out of the shower twenty minutes later, wrapped in the most decadent bath towel she'd ever experienced.

"Vegas," Marlo froze in the doorway. "I just gotta' know." Ivy sat on her bed with that *Oh-this-should-be-good* grin of hers. She held up the credit card skimmer Marlo had hidden on the underside of the molded chip tray like it was a mouse hanging by the tail. "What the hell?"

"Not what you think, Ivy." She moved to grab the skimmer and Ivy moved out of reach. "It's all part of a security check." She tightened her towel. Ivy was dancing around the room like a little kid. "Just wait...let me get dressed." Margo ducked behind the bathroom door and pulled on yoga pants and an oversized t-shirt with VEGAS in bright silver sequins across her chest.

This time when she came out Ivy held up the ear buds she'd buried even deeper.

"Any other fun stuff in there?" Ivy teased. "You don't expect me to believe the whole security check thing, do you?"

Marlo was caught, and worse yet, if Ivy figured out how to connect the com system to Cy, then she'd ruined his future, too.

"Oh, relax, will ya." Ivy tossed it all on the bed and sat down in the chair. "If it's even half of what I think it is, these folks have had it coming for years. I just want to be around when they find out they've been taken." She popped her legs across the arm of the chair and kicked off her tennis shoes. "Come on, dish."

Number three on the list: Be ready to improvise at a moment's notice. Check.

Marlo crossed back to the black pants lying on the bathroom floor and dug out the copy LTN Ministries had sent her mother and handed it to Ivy. She finished the dregs of the beer she stole from the bar while Ivy read.

"Bastards," Ivy said. She handed the letter back to Marlo. "Who is this Beverly Compton to you?"

"She's my mom...Bev. She has stage three breast

cancer, and she gave them a huge part of her savings to buy into this plan." Marlo refused to cry again. "She lost her house, her savings, everything."

Ivy chewed her lip for a few seconds while Marlo weighed the pros and cons of tackling her, tying her up, and putting her in the closet. No rope. Okay...

"I'm in. What's the next step?"

"Uh, no, Ivy. No. Thanks, but this has the potential to go way off the rails, and I've already got one guy looking at prison time if I screw up."

"Cy?"

"How did you..."

"I heard you talking in the parking lot before we went through security," Ivy said.

"Uh, huh..." Marlo was at a total loss for what came next. It was clear Ivy wasn't going to fade out.

"Look, Ivy, I don't want you mixed up in this, and I can't pay you. This money is already going to some people who really need it." Ivy cocked her head to the side and listened. "But there is one part that you could help with that would give me piece of mind."

"Go on..."

Marlo decided to come clean. "I was sure Reb would use his personal credit card, but he didn't. Being the upstanding guy that he is, he used the company account. That means he gave us access to all of it." Ivy's eyes bugged out.

* * *

The second day was as gorgeous as the first. Marlo didn't notice. She'd been up all night going back and forth about trusting Ivy and wondering if she should chance pulling out the earbuds Cy had given her for emergency contact.

They should ditch the plan.

If the bleach twins hadn't shown up at her door, it probably meant Ivy had kept her word. It could also mean they were bluffing, waiting to see what else she had planned and who was helping.

She set up the table according to the schedule and waited. Ivy gave her a wink and snuck her a crystal tumbler full of whiskey on the sly just before everyone moved to the forward deck. Tikis lit and everyone seated, Marlo announced the game. An hour in, she began to notice Travis sneaking glances at Reb and Reb grinning slightly. She was sure they were about to spring on her.

Reb tapped his check with four fingers and Travis smiled. Now she understood, Travis and Reb were working together to run the table. She cleared her throat and raised an eyebrow at Reb.

"Ah, come on now Vegas." He laughed a little, turning on the good ol' boy charm. "You've heard the saying *good for the game*, right?" Reb threw in two purple chips and upped the bet.

"Yes, sir. I have."

"What's that mean?" asked the newest member of the Howard team, Tom Jacobs.

"It's a term used in the poker community that implies sometimes we should look the other way when things get a bit shady so the game can continue with a good reputation," Marlo answered. "But we're all about playing fair and good family values, right Mr. Howard?"

"Right, Vegas. That's who we are. Absolutely." Reb reordered the cards he was holding and grabbed his beer. Travis frowned and held up another thousand dollar chip for her to see, baiting her.

The captain ran onto the deck and whispered something into Reb's ear. The color drained from his face. Marlo looked over at the bar and spotted Ivy, who nodded. Seconds later, alarms began to sound.

Reb stood. "Ladies and gentlemen," he bellowed. Please make your way to the life boats. This is not a drill. The crew have found an explosive device on board, and we need to evacuate immediately."

All hell broke loose. Everyone was yelling and tripping over the person in front of them as the race for the stairs began. The crew had already begun opening the life rafts. Marlo reached up into her hair and took out the earbuds tapping the button on the side to power up.

"Cy, you should have received transmission of all accounts by now." She paused and grinned at Ivy. "Then I think we're a go," she whispered.

Within ten minutes everyone made it to the lifeboats, and they were putting distance between them and the ship. The Coast Guard had been notified, but before they arrived, the blast shook the *Love Thy Neighbor* and pieces rained down in the dark Florida water.

Reb Howard stood up and watched his prized ship, launched piece by piece into the sky. Just then his phone pinged with an email from his bank showing the new company account balance, and he roared. At the same time, a bank transfer to an account in the Caymans ensured that very soon, every member of the LTN Ministries had their investment returned and outstanding medical bills paid.

Ivy held up a fist to Marlo and laughed.

Ursula Vogt writes from the Piedmont Region of the Southern Appalachians. She grew up on stories of hard times and harder decisions, including her grandparents "running shine" through the coal mines of Southern Kansas. She writes both crime noir and traditional thrillers with relatable characters you'll likely recognize as the family down the street, or the guy you went to high school with. She is a trained court reporter turned professional copywriter, teaches GED Prep, and writes stories about average people and deadly decisions. You can read more short stories under her pen name, Ella Ahrens, at Shotgun Honey (https://shotgunhoney.com/fiction/house-warming-by-ella-ahrens/). Follow Ursula's most current projects at UrsulaVogt.com

The Final Word

Did you enjoy this anthology? Then please leave an honest review on Amazon. Reviews help sell books by putting us higher on the Amazon algorithm and by telling others what you liked about the book.

And, which story was your favorite? Consider following that author and seeing if they have other stories you'd love.

And, check out Volume one of the anthology! Find ThrillHers with your favorite online retailer.

or search for 'ThrillHers Sonja Dewing".